BAD BOY BOOGIE

The Adventures of Bon Scott

With an Introduction
by John Kinsella

SHED UNDER THE MOUNTAIN

First published 2017 by Shed Under The Mountain

SHED UNDER THE MOUNTAIN

ISBN-13: 978-0980477047

ISBN-10: 0980477042

For Rosie

Contents

INTRODUCTION
by John Kinsella

Listening to the *Highway to Hell* album, especially the track 'Night Prowler', I know I am with Bon at his most intense, warped and sublime. And I know this because of his voice, his lyrics, and what would shortly become of his life. Ended. And reading the final incarnation of J. P. Quinton's novel 'on' or 'about' Bon, I know I am in something akin to that feeling I get listening to that great album, that song.

I was there for the entire journey when James first described the book he wanted to write — the picaresque of a unique rock singer's life, but also the life's journey of someone who partly grew up in the zone of habitation Quinton and I both know. This would be a novel about place, an individual, and a time. J. P. Quinton is younger, but I was eleven when AC/

DC hit it big in Australia. I know this journey and I know the stomping ground. Quinton has 'travelled' with Bon and made it a universal story of threat, in-your-face challenge, ambition, desire, lust, migration, class, learning, breaking convention, and music... rock and roll!

'Night Prowler' is a disturbing song that relishes being disturbing. This is beyond the bad-boy image of the rocker; it's malevolent. On the other hand, for those of you who've read some of Bon's letters, especially his 'love' letters (onanistic and ironic and pleading and distancing and humorous and sad at once), you'll know that what Bon projects into the persona of singer, of rocker, and who he actually was, slipped back and forth, was as stable as alcohol can't allow you to be. Bon broke rules; he took a 'criminal' rebel psychology to his music, and maybe his sexuality, but he also took pathos and caring. It's a complex picture, and this is why, maybe, his story is best told in fiction rather than biography. It's something that can't be biographised.

When Quinton was working out the 'scenes' around which his novel would revolve, he took incidents from Bon's life-journey, a Huckleberry-Finn-crossed-with-Alvin-Purple approach, and brought them together with an understanding of place — especially Fremantle and Perth and the band's early days in 'the East' and London. Temporal and spatial markers of Bon's life merge with often stunning portraits of a period in a sliver of 'Australian life', especially the life of a migrant. Tension between the official version of what it is to be 'Australian' and the reality for a Scottish migrant in Fremantle drives the early part of the narrative.

This is a story of teenage years, of growing towards adulthood in a confused, compromised, and troubled way, but with a strong compulsion to change the conditions of one's life. In a remarkable scene, Quinton takes us inside Riverbank detention centre and creates a dialogue between an indigenous inmate and the migrant, Bon. This is a construct, but a feasible one, and illuminating of time and place. Further, Quinton shows us his skill at going inside his character's psyche, as we look at a contradictory world through Bon's eyes.

I can attest to the amount of research that J. P. Quinton undertook, not only regarding Bon's life story, but around the history of blues music and the deviation of AC/DC's and Bon's version of rock and roll. This is not the complete story of Bon's life; it's a series of scenes starting in Fremantle and catching salient 'moments' in the biography and fictionalised imagining of his life. We are given glimpses into what makes Bon's character tick; how this feeds into the public idea of who we think he is.

Quinton spent much time interviewing whoever he could find who had known Bon — from casual acquaintances to some of those who had been closest to him. Bon was capable of great love and affection, and the women who were vital in his 'real life' remain vital in the life we imagine for him. So much of it is about loss in the sense of lives that can't synch. Bon loved more than he could manage relationships. We get a sense of that here, without the novel ever intruding into the private space/s of others. Which brings us to the question of whether or not this is a work of intrusion, a work that goes where one shouldn't go. I think not — it takes biographical details and makes fiction.

The question of 'voice' is vital to this book — how it shifts and how 'deep' into the character it is going, or how it is coming out. The tone and register of language are vital. For example, regarding phrasing: bring to mind the talk on 1950s/60s music shows to get the feel of the language; there's also the flavour of 1970s rock magazines, *Rolling Stone*, *Ram* from Australia, etc. 'Setting' in terms of the era, the place as it was, is created through meetings of language and place. The shift from talking about the murderer Eric Edgar Cooke to Bon talking about 'Hell' is unnerving. It is difficult to tie 'real-life' events, especially something so horrific, into the narrative without being gratuitous and creating bathos, but I think in *The Adventures of Bon Scott*, its ironic (sad) title resonating, Quinton does it just enough. Never too much. The same applies to how much of the 'characters' who intersect with Bon's life should be revealed, how rounded they can actually afford to be in the story, especially with Bon's 'main' love, Silver.

In some ways, *The Adventures of Bon Scott* does venture into those private spaces which are no one's business, not even for an 'official' biographer of a living person, but it does so through literature, through creating a character who inflects the human condition. In Bon's character are good and bad, success and failure, selfishness and caring. It's a complex portrait, which might, in different ways and different degrees, be applied to many people in their own circumstances. Bon's life was different from most of our lives, but he was a very human boy and a very human man who struggled towards completeness and maturity through so many external as well as internal socio-economic and cultural circumstances. His is a story of slipping between the planks, but also of having family, and his own certitudes. If he's done wrong, it's not necessarily for the reasons the rest of the world thinks he has done wrong. Certainly not the 'system', as the brilliant court scene in the novel conveys.

In chatting with J. P. Quinton over the years of his writing this book, I recall his various recountings of meetings with those who knew Bon. I particularly relished his interviewing

Molly Meldrum, who has been such a figure for many of us interested in the journey of Australian rock music. The Meldrum public persona, the music impresario, came across in this recounting, and somehow such encounters inform one of the important layers of fictional realism in this book — a matter of tone. James gets the tone so often spot-on for a generation.

For any reader of Bon's life, the band AC/DC is going to be at the core. And it is, in this novel, or what I would call a 'fictionalisation'. But the essential nature of it is revealed in Bon's interaction with the remarkable character of Angus Young. Angus is bizarrely mentored into experience (of a sort) by Bon, but is also a model of discipline, dedication and musical obsessiveness for Bon. Angus means business. Angus has his own world in his head, and it doesn't accord with a world outside rock and roll. Angus and Bon kind of *get* each other. There's a sharing in there, beneath all the complexities of the trying to 'make it' as a band, that is touching and sensitive.

Bon is obsessed with sex. Not just as a means of physical pleasure, but as a means of connection, of alleviating his own inner loneliness. On the road, he thinks over his stuffed-up relationships, and of those he truly loves. He regrets his behaviours and addictions, but is also strangely happy with who he is. Quinton sets up a series of sexual encounters that convey much more than lust, and skilfully critique gender mores and inequalities of the time without telling the reader what's what. A lot of things are implied by setting and swift changes in scenery (especially when the police are closing in!). And where there's humour, there's often something troubling in multifaceted and murky ways.

This is not a work of judgement, but of exploration: of looking into and out of the mind and emotions of a unique and conflicted individual. We see the world through Bon's eyes, but not only from Bon's point of view. It takes mastery to carry this, and I feel Quinton has created a unique mode of making fiction reach where biography can't by looking into what makes the human, flawed and resplendent at once.

One thing I am wary of in any fictionalising of the 'rock life' is creating a set of vignettes without real narrative connection. I feel Quinton has avoided doing this. What he has done is show us something closer to the *Confessions* Augustine might have written if he had not (yet) found God. There's something of the Australian grunge novel in this work, but other maybe stronger influences from writers of the nouveau roman such as Robbe-Grillet, as J. P. Quinton has plenty of inherent grunge in himself! What's interesting about this book as experimental narrative is that it's like many styles and movements coalescing in the life of one who was in essence many styles, movements and even personalities. And the essence of this novel is its ability to be more than a combination of true confessions, rockumentary, and snippets into the working of a soul.

What J. P. Quinton had to search for in the writing of this work was the growth in Bon as character, and I think he found that. I think the reader, in some ways, needs to forget about this character being 'Bon Scott' and let him be, well, a character moving towards something. I think of Carson McCullers — her characters might not 'progress', but they do 'change', and some imagine epiphanies. The events of their lives shift the way they are inside. But writing a new work in a new 'style' with a mind to how Bon Scott's many fans, and his many friends, might feel, comes with pitfalls. Without labouring the point, and while retaining the 'adventurous' spirit of the work — its 'Alvin Purple' picturesque twang — I think that Quinton has skilfully managed to negotiate these pitfalls of rock and roll 'melodrama', and has opened new ground for such works.

This novel is about energy — how it is thwarted, and how it needs to find release. 'Night Prowler' is not Bon, yet Bon's lyrics show how effectively he could inhabit a persona. On stage, he became the characters he sang out of — in this remarkable novel, Bon's persona is inhabited by a version of Bon himself. We are with him because we have seen him on stage and heard him on record, and we have seen how he comports himself, how he becomes one with music and lyrics and stage. When in 'TNT' Bon sings, 'So lock up your daughter. Lock up your wife...', he is not speaking for the sexual repression of women, but of the nature of sexual repression in patriarchal society keeping 'its' womenfolk under surveillance. With tongue in cheek (almost), he is offering his own form of liberation. Bon as deliverance. Vehicle and tenor.

Bon is an event. A *mostly* ironic event. And this book is an event in which Bon is given a textual stage on which to enact one of his — no, many of his — personae. And as I speak of his lyrics, I am reminded of the real Bon and the fictionalised Bon, and I am further reminded — as a jolt to myself — of the brilliant lyrics J.P. Quinton wrote through his character Bon when working on this book. Bon Scott would have given them lives they didn't even know they had. And in the end, it's the loss of life that underpins the tragedy of his life. And of this novel's protagonist, 'Bon Scott'.

John Kinsella, Jam Tree Gully, 2016

LIST OF CHARACTERS

ROCK 'N' ROLL SINGER:

Derek - Bon's younger brother
Mark and Darren - hill racers
Terry - Bon's teenage mate, bass player in The Spektors
Isa - Bon's mum
Suzy - Bon's first girlfriend - secretary of The Spektors
Betty - Terry's sister
Cunstable Taylor - Bon's police nemesis
Norman - Bon's cellmate
Monkey - Riverbank security guard

THE VALENTINES:

Vince - co-singer
Ted - bass
Wyn - guitar
Paddy - drummer
Darc - roadie
Gabby - Darc's girlfriend
Charmaine - art student
Vicki - next door neighbour, and later
Uncle's ex-girlfriend in Fraternity
Julianna - check out chick
Ian (Molly) Meldrum - music journalist

FRATERNITY:

Bruce - bass
Uncle - harmonica
J.B. - keyboard
Mick - guitar
John - drums

Pat Pickett - mate from Melbourne - and
later roadie (spider) for AC/DC
Ralph - roadie (spider)
Richard - government bureaucrat
Irene - Bon's wife
Len and Carol - couple at Port Pirie pub
Port Pirie police - Holt, Mackenzie, Jones and Roberts

AC/DC, GONE SHOOTIN', BAD BOY BOOGIE, HIGHWAY TO HELL:

Angus - guitar
Malcolm - guitar, Angus' older brother
Mark - bass
Phil - drums
Michael Browning - manager
Kate - groupie
Judy - Bon's fling
Ozzy - singer from Black Sabbath
Leroy Kincaid - revolutionary
Silver Smith - Bon's girlfriend in London
Gerard - Germany Tour Coordinator
Cliff - bass player after Mark
Ahmet - owner of Atlantic records
Alistair - Silver's friend

ROCK 'N' ROLL SINGER

Fremantle — 1962

I blame school. All this sitting still, the same old stuff, over and over again. It's like some old bastard's version of *hell* for kids. As soon as the bell rings I run to the primary school where my little brother Dereck is picking his bag out of the pile on the verandah. We walk home over Stirling Highway bridge, stopping to watch the boats slip by and the ships get loaded.

"Anyone pick on your accent today?" I ask him, as he climbs on the white railing, his hair blown flat.

"No, Miss Sidebottom won't let 'em," he says, squinting into the sun. Rods and lines flick back and forward beneath us. I've been in detention a few times for fighting with the other kids for the way I speak. Mum says to ignore them and come straight home. Where the two highways join I see a few kids carrying sheets of tin, the good ones from the Matilda Bay brewery bin. They're heading for the big hill. There hasn't been any rain for a few weeks so the grass will be fast. I send Dereck home and run to catch them.

Me, Darren, the stevedore's kid, and his little brother Mark walk by the brick houses with lemon and olive trees out front. We're all puffing by the time we get to the top, struggling with the tin in the wind, trying not to cut our hands. The park is a long rectangle that droops in one corner and lifts up at the other, like a raised bed sheet. You can belt all the way to the house fences at the bottom, but everyone normally rolls off on the flatter bit in the middle.

There are other kids here, from the across the river. One kid named Terry, an Aussie kid I've seen at school. An old lady sits in the sun watching us. The port towers trail off in the distance. A couple of magpies walk around, digging in the dirt.

"Race ya," says Terry, flicking his chin up. "Us two against you three, first one to the fence." I look at Darren and Mark. Mark is ready, Darren doesn't look so sure.

"I'll race you myself," I say, grabbing the tin off Darren, putting it on the cusp of the hill. Mark doesn't say anything. He jumps behind me and grabs my belly. We bump forward a little, my feet outside the tin. "Lie back and hold on tight," I tell him. We move forward again, the drop scary.

Darren, sitting in behind the other kid yells, "On your marks, get set," I pull the edges back, "go." I see the ocean and the houses and then I'm facing the grass and the whirring in my ears gets louder. Mark grabs me tight, his cheek on my back. I nearly lose grip on the tin as we get to the lump and then the steep bit starts, we're beating them.

I yell to Mark to lean forward. The tin gets hot through my shorts. They gain on us but there's not far to go, we're gunna win. We start to veer right and they start to veer left. They're gaining and they're right on us but there's no way to stop. They smash into us, the tin getting caught in the ground when I let go. I put my feet up and kick Terry in the back and he slams into the fence and Darren crashes into us.

Dust gets in our hair and teeth. I stand up and I'm about to ask Darren if he's alright. I can see grass burns all over the bottom of his back when someone hits me hard and slams me to the ground. I'm in a head lock. I can't breathe and then I'm ripped up and flung over and kicked in the head.

"Whadya smash into us for you idiot?" he says.

"You smashed into us," I say, my ears burning, my back itchy, blood dribbling from my elbow. My shirt is ripped.

"Race you again and see who won, fair and square," he says. We start walking up the hill. Darren follows me and he smiles when I tell him he'll be alright.

"Try and get me in a headlock again and you're dead," I say, bits of sand in my mouth.

"Kick me in the back again and I'll flatten you." We set up our racing sheets and immediately he and the other kid hop on. Mark doesn't want to go again, and stands there shaking.

"What's ya mate, a sissy?" says Terry, half his face covered in dirt.

"Get on, Mark, *get on*," I say. As soon as I feel his arms around me, I'm off, I don't wait. Terry and Darren must have the same idea because by the time we hit the lump we're neck and neck. I lean forward and go flat out. I'm not stopping this time. The wooden fence is getting closer and we're winning. I look back and they've rolled off. Then the fence is on us I pull the sheet up but it's too late. Everything goes dark and we tumble and we hit the fence hard.

I get to my feet and Mark has landed between me and the fence and he's lying there in a heap and he's bawling his eyes out and twisting on the ground, banging his legs into the fence like he's having a fit, making an awful sound. He gets up holding one arm with the other, his face blood red, tears streaming and his chin all wrinkled. I try to help him but he starts running and all these people are coming from their houses and I know he's broken his arm and I know it's my fault and word gets around quick and I'm supposed to go straight home after school so I start running toward the river up the hill by the water tower and then down through the paperbarks into the black sand. I keep running along the shore in the cold shade of the trees hanging out over the water. I keep running until I'm out of breath.

In the cave there are lolly wrappers and a pile of ashes where some big kids must have had a fire. I can't breathe properly and wish I had my puffer. Tiny black flies fill the holes in the cave ceiling. Out the cave opening I see tree tops and yachts and fast moving clouds. I hear the clang of factories and a few seagulls. By the time my breath slows enough for me to not hear it there's voices outside. I poke my head out and when I see it's Terry I call for him to come up. You gotta climb between two big rocks to get inside and I move over to let him in.

"You know him?" Terry asks.

'Who?"

"The crying kid, dummy."

"Not so much," I say, "but I'll get in trouble anyway." He shifts forward onto his knees and pulls out a small red tin from his pocket and pries it open with his dirty fingers.

"Tried this stuff before?" he asks, lighting a match. He brings the flame to the white tip and begins drawing on and off. Flies stir overhead. The end grows brighter and brighter and he takes a lung full and grabs the base with thumb and forefinger and hands it to me like a pair of scissors. I hesitate.

"Here," he says, sounding distant. The paper feels strange, the stick wobbling in my fingers. I take a draw and the other end fires up, veins turning black. The feeling of acid exploding in my throat like toxic confetti. I start coughing. I try to stop but can't. He grabs my hand and takes the joint back. Spit fills my mouth. I swallow. "You get used to it," he says, sucking back on it like he's done it a thousand times before.

His dark eyes go glossy. His lips curl at either end as he half winces. He hands the joint back and I have another go and cough violently again, the taste like dirt and vegetables and ash. Then my hands and feet start tingling, then my arms and shoulders and then my head. A new feeling, tingling all over making my legs light, my scalp itchy.

"Give me the thing," he says, so I hand it back and he says I *Swanny Rivered* it. But he keeps sucking away and then I feel tickling on the outside of my arm and think it's a spider or something so I flick and twist and jump and bash my head on the rocks and Terry starts giggling. I kick up dust and rub my head and hear more seagull noises.

"Thought it was a waps, or a bee," I say, settling back.

"Waps, what's a waps?"

"You know what I mean, there's wasp nests all around here."

"Yeah I can't stand those wasps, sting me on my k-nee." I look over at him and see him warm and grinning. *BUZZZZzzzzzz* in my mouth the sound the zeds like small wooden blocks. I buzz until I can buzz no more and run my sweaty palms over rocks.

"The sun's almost gone," he says, lying with his legs folded. "If I had a blanket I'd sleep here tonight, too many people at my place." I see a tattoo under his shirt sleeve and ask him where he got it.

"Got a mate in Vic Park, gives me a special price." He rolls his sleeve up to show me a snarling panther in grass.

"Did it hurt?"

"At the time, but only a little bit, like gettin' bit by a bull ant."

"My dad's got a few tatts," I say.

"Wanna get one with me?" He lights another match and holds the end until the flame goes out and he doesn't flinch from the burning. "We'll find some money somewhere and drive to Vic Park on Saturday. After we can go to Port Beach with my sister Betty, you'll like her."

"What? For the Johnny Young show?"

"Yeah, you know it?"

"I sing sometimes, in the breaks. But I wanna play drums."

"Really?" He sits up all excited. "We're starting a band, me and my mates, we're called The Spektors, after Phil Spector, but spelt with a K. Wanna join us?"

"Hell yeah man." He gets up and walks out of the cave and I follow, keeping my head drooped.

"We'll practise at my place on Petra Street."

"Okay." He looks me in the eyes.

"If you're worried about your parents seeing your red eyes go for a swim and say you opened them underwater. Ever jumped off the cliffs stoned?"

"Never been stoned."

"Oh really," his eyebrows raise. "You forget who you are. Better than sex."

"Never had sex," I say.

"What are ya? Some kind of poof?"

"No. I do naughty stuff all the time."

"Oh yeah, like what." We keep walking on the dirt tracks, the light getting less and less.

"I let grenades go in the river," I say.

"Big deal, I rolled a boulder on railway tracks. Then when I flagged the train down, they gave me a reward."

"You know about the fish heads in the swimming pool?" He shrugs his shoulders.

"You know the big white rich house near the water tower?" he asks, letting the branch of a tree fling in my face.

"Yeah."

"I smashed all the windows."

"You know the Weetbix factory?" I ask.

"Yep."

"I blew the hole in the wall."

"You never?" He flings his head.

"Police came to my house and questioned me and everything," I say.

Terry leads me beneath peppermint smelling trees and we climb up white rocks with broken glass in the gaps. We pull ourselves up by tree branches worn smooth by hands. The ridge, like a small patch of the moon's surface, is about ten yards above the water. We strip off and the fast wind makes our skin cold and the water lumpy.

Terry has another tattoo of a lion on his back. He throws his shirt on top of his little red tin, climbs up on a mound, outstretches his arms, bends his knees and jumps. My eyes follow his fall and he breaks the water with a clap, the water green to dark blue from the shore outward. He disappears in bubbles and emerges breaststroking as far as you can throw a rock away. "*YYYEEEOOOOO,*" he yells and the people in the dinghy nearby start watching.

I crawl to the edge, keeping my weight low, letting my hands do the work. I crouch low on top of the mound with both hands either side. "The more you think about it, the harder it gets," he yells, but his voice sounds different from the water. My heart starts going as I look out and don't know if I can jump far enough to avoid the rocks. A gust of wind fills my mouth. There's a patch of dirt big enough to slip on that I dig my toes in. I don't put my arms out. I don't fully stand, I launch myself outwards, my legs folded like a shield to the air. I'm falling and falling faster, no control. I feel my insides move upward inside my skin. The air loud. Louder than the tin race. The water big, bigger.

Boosh, my feet and shins and bum crash through the surface and I don't open my eyes. My ears explode and my nose fills with water and I swim as fast as possible up to the top. I blow my nose clean and my hearing returns with a pop. My arms move in the bubbles that float upstream in the current. I lay back and clap water up and see the pink clouds, thin and high, and want some more joint.

Terry swims back and climbs up to the top. I see his head and he yells out, "Seeya tomorra, Bon," and walks off tip toeing on the rocks. I feel scared all of a sudden and climb back and get dressed and begin the long walk home, singing to myself, the lights coming on around the bay, my stomach rumbling. I hold my shoes with two fingers and try to avoid rocks and sticks, losing my balance and knowing Mum and Dad are going to be real annoyed. The weed has worn off. Feeling has returned to my fingertips and I cup my breath in my hand and have a whiff.

I sing some Elvis and use the shampoo bottle as a microphone, really in the groove, hitting the notes bouncing off the tiles. I wash my new tattoo, a pair of sparrows nesting in a love heart below my belly button. *Well it's a...*

"*Ron, Ron,*" Mum sticks her head in the door. She has a thicker Scottish accent than me. "Don't use all th'a hot water."

"Okay Mum," I say, spitting soapy water out my mouth.

"And sing like yerself, ye might be Doris Day, but yer no Elvis."

"Get out Mum."

"Spoke tae yer teacher too, she says ye've not been at school."

"I hate school."

"What else ye gonna do?" I don't answer, hoping she'll go away. "You've got th' Empire Games this Sunday, don't forget. Your Father an' yer brother are coming. Don't ignore yer brothers, they have every right—"

"I wasn't Mum, can you wait until I'm done?"

"Don't argue Ron. Ye canne ignore them. Ye ne'er play with them. We hardly see you. We don't know what ye up too. This Night Prowler is out there killing folk, an' we don't know where ye are. The police came to yer father's work an' took fingerprints."

"I'm not a bloody murderer Mum."

"I know, but I don't like the thought ay ye gettin' hurt."

"*Get out.*" She closes the door. I dry off and go to make my way to my room, but she grabs my arm.

"Yer grandparents are coming soon."

"You've told me a thousand times," I shake out of her grip.

"They'll be stayin' in Dereck's room. He'll be sharing yer room."

At the bottom of Harvest Road there's a market garden, a couple of factories and some mechanics shops with car yards. The footpaths are crushed limestone and they dirty my polished shoes. After crossing the highway I take goat trails over weedy lots. There's a musty wool smell from the sheds that makes me sneeze. I've just enough to buy a bottle of Stone's but I have to find someone to buy it for me. I wait in the car park at the Railway Hotel and up creeps this massive orange light over the line of trees back way beyond the train bridge. Either a big plane or someones shifted the port over to the east.

Two women walking their dogs approach and agree to buy the bottle for me. I wait with one of them on the street, thinking of what to say, looking up at the moon full and bursting like a blemished orange. The lady gives me the bottle in a brown paper bag and says to share it and they take the path back to the highway through the dunes. I stop on the tracks and take a swig of the sweet tang and see white sand stalking the petrol silo curves. Multicoloured lights emanate from the concrete surf club, the Port Beach Stomp. I hear bits and bobs of music, same songs Johnny Young always plays.

I try to kill my nervous energy with the Stone's ginger ale. I exhale and take another scull. Squeeze the bottle hard in my hand. There's the ocean behind the buildings and the crash of waves and a brown panel van snakes between the sheoaks, its headlights on high beam blinding me. "Watcha looking at?" the guy in the passenger seat asks but I don't answer, I slide the bottle into my undies against my tattoo and go inside.

The walls are lined with green steel chairs and tables. A couple of girls stand around chatting and pointing at people on the dance floor, a mass of limbs and hair flying. Up the back the band plays on a small platform under cellophane covered flood lights. A tap on my shoulder. Betty wearing tight jeans, high heels, a polka dot blouse knotted at the front. With her is a girl I've never seen before, her lips and cheeks red.

"You know Suzy, don't ya?" We shake hands awkwardly. "She's the president of the Spektors fan club," says Betty. Her blond hair covers the right side of her face, her skin soft and white. Her voice has an accent I've never heard before and she leans in so I can hear her over the band.

"I hear you're the new drummer." The warmth of her neck and the smell of vanilla. I get shy.

"We'll have to wait and see."

"You gunna sing tonight, Bonny?" asks Betty.

"Hope so. If Johnny lets me."

"He won't have a choice. We'll make him, won't we, Suzy?" She smiles at me and then turns to the band.

"Where's Terry?" I ask.

"He's on his way. Jesus, you boys are joined at the hip. C'mon, let's dance." She pulls me along and I grab Suzy's hand and the bottle in my pants hurts. I pull it out and take a swig, and offer it to the girls.

While we're dancing we start pointing to each other --singing the words to one another--shaking our bums and wagging our fingers. We work our way to the middle as more people leave. The band is coming to the end of their first set. Up the front are more of Betty's friends jiving their hearts out. The song slows and fades and Johnny announces a break. Suzy goes up on stage and up to the microphone and takes out a sheet of paper.

"Excuse me everybody." She's short, and you can hardly see her even on stage. Everyone starts chatting and no one listens and she tries again.

"Shut up," yells Betty, but no one listens to her either. The crowd gets louder and no one takes any notice of her so I jump on stage and take her elbow, gentle.

"Hey, hey, listen here, listen people. You lot up the back," I say, squinting in the lights. One of them points to himself. "Yeah, you and your mates, can you listen in for a second?" The crowd goes quiet and Suzy looks up at me and she's beautiful and her sheet of paper is shaking.

"The Spektors will be playing at the Kwinana Town Hall next Saturday starting at six p.m. Posters will be placed around town. Thank you."

"Yeah and Bonnie is the new drummer," yells Betty and then her and her friends start chanting, *Bonnie, Bonnie, Bonnie,* clapping and jumping trying to get me to sing a song. Some of the band members return to their instruments and Johnny, being a good sport, comes back on and introduces me. I close my eyes and see Mum telling me to sing like myself and try not to sound like anyone else. She sings in the Scottish club, so she knows about this stuff. I can feel everyone watching me, some willing me to stuff up. The band already knows I like *Blue Suede Shoes* so they launch into that. As we reach the crescendo someone throws a bra on stage and I whip it over my shoulder like a tea towel and pull the microphone off the stand and let rip for the finale.

The song ends and the girls start chanting my name again, but the boys want a break. I step off stage and rejoin the huddle. I feel a pinch on my bum and turn quick and catch Suzy.

"You're really good. You're a natural," she says, pushing her bracelets up her arm.

"Feel like going for a walk?" I ask her.

"No."

"Come on, just along the beach a bit."

"What for?"

"Just to get some fresh air."

Outside are some boys in blue I've seen around but they don't see us and we walk through the car park and the gang in the panel van don't see us either. After the soft sand of the path we walk along the water's edge. Lines of seaweed follow the curve of the water. The moon is high and full and the sand is the same colour as the moon. We struggle up the dune and I take my jacket off, pull the Stones bottle out.

"See the Rottnest lighthouse?" she asks, pointing to the horizon. I just want to kiss her. "We learnt in school you could walk to Rottnest not long ago."

"When, last week?"

"No, silly, ten thousand years ago."

"I got a tattoo," I tell her.

"A tattoo, why on earth would you get a tattoo?"

"Something to do, I guess. Wanna see it?" I stand up and undo my fly. I turn to face the moonlight.

"Did it hurt?"

"Yeah, like hell."

"Can I touch?" Her cold slender finger traces the outline. I shiver and she giggles. I grab her hand and sit back down. I lean in to kiss her.

"I've never kissed anyone before," she says.

"Neither have I."

"Ha. Sure, Bon. I've heard about you."

"What?"

"Things." She turns away. Her armpits over her knees. She turns back and I peck her on the cheek. My dick is bouncing around in my undone jeans. I move her hair out the way and kiss her neck, hairspray smell and warm skin. She pulls on my shirt with one hand and lightly tugs my hair. I hear her breathe. With my left hand I cup her boob and feel the wire in her bra. She grabs my hand.

"I'm not sure, Bon," her voice soft. A car engine roars behind us.

"Neither am I," I say, laughing. She rests her forehead on mine and we brush noses. Breathing deep, my shoulders rise, and I feel nervous again. I unscrew the bottle cap and take a swig. She doesn't have any.

"Maybe next time, Bonnie." She pushes her feet, making a pyramid in the sand.

"You been to any of the clubs in the city?"

"Not yet. Our family has a farm near Bridgetown and we usually go away for the holidays, but I want to stay in town this time."

"I'll take you." We get up and start walking back. In the car park is the panel van, some guy pissing and stumbling nearby. I grab Suzy's hand and start walking faster, the club about 100 yards away. Two of them follow us and we get closer but then one comes out of the club and starts walking our way. He's not so big and stupid enough looking. We go to walk around him but he blocks our path, so we switch back and he stops us. I pull the old fake-punch-to-the-face, whack-em-hard-in-the-stomach trick and don't look back. We go inside as casual as can be. I find Betty as quick as I can. She's dancing the twist with some geezer.

"Betty, Betty, where's Terry?"

"I don't know, he's not here yet I don't think."

"Didn't he say he was coming?"

"Yeah, he always does, doesn't he? He was fixing his car when I left." In the doorway I see one of the panel van kids pointing the cops our way.

"If you see him, tell him I'm looking for him."

"What's going on, Bon?"

"No big deal, make sure Suzy stays with you." During the day you can get out through the dunny block but they lock it at night. The only other exit is out the deliveries door through the kiosk, but that'll be locked too and old Rex will tell the boys in blue if I poke my head in. Only other option is to hide in the ladies for a while and sneak out when the band finishes.

I cover up my face with my hair and sneak in after a bunch of girls come out and go in a cubicle and lock the door. Everything is concrete except the bog roll holder and toilet seat and paint is coming away from the floor and the fluoro lights are covered in bugs. There's tear drop shaped piles of wet sand leading to the drain pipes. The smell of seaweed is strong and makes me need to chuck a shit. About four or five girls enter and none of them use the loos, they chat away. I'm about half way done when all the chatter stops.

"Excuse me ladies. Everybody out." One of the cops. I recognise his voice. Oh, you've got to be joking, it's Cuntsable Taylor, the one who questioned me about blowing a hole in the Weetbix factory. A thud on each door and creaking. "If there's anyone in here don't be alarmed, it's the police". I'm in the end cubicle and I lift my feet up and I can see his black boots. He taps on the door.

"Everything alright in there?" I put on my best female voice, which isn't hard for me.

"MMyes, I have an upset stomach."

"That sure seems to be the case, miss."

"Won't be too much longer."

"You take your time, we're looking for a boy by the name of Ron, or Bon. You seen him?"

"No." I cough. "Never heard of him. What does he look like?"

"A real short ass. Brown wavy hair, big nose, bit stupid looking. Why don't you open the door and I'll help you. You feeling sick?" The perv, he opens the door and I'll throttle him. Bet he helps out young girls all the time.

"I'm fine, nearly finished."

"Alright, Miss, you see him you come tell me." He starts walking out. I wait a few minutes reading the scratches on the wall. *Elspeth is a slut. Wayne Smith has a big dick. Tanya was ere. C.S.L.S.C are shit.* With my pocket knife I add my own little poem.

A NOD MEANS YEP
TWO SHAKES MEANS NOT
IF MY PANTS STICK OUT
SHE GOT WHAT I GOT.

The band stops and I figure this is a good time to sneak out. I wash my hands and make sure my hair looks good. I check my teeth and catch a patch of blue in the mirror and then there's a caning feeling on my neck and Cuntsable Taylor drags me into one of the cubicles. He grabs my collar and jams his fist into my throat.

"Bon-bloody-Scott. Thought I'd catch you in here you little weevil. I know you've been in the dunes with an underaged girl. I know you punched young Stewart in the car park." With every statement he slams me against the wall. "And what's this?" He pulls the Stone's bottle out, throws it in the toilet.

"We've crossed paths before, and I've got your number sonny. I know you blew the hole in the Weeties factory wall. I could tell you were lying," he says.

"Weetbix."

"What?"

"It was the Weetbix factory, not Weeties, there's no Weeties factory in Freo." He frowns. He doesn't get it.

"Now I catch you in the ladies. One day when I catch you in the act I'm taking you to the station and you can sing to an empty cell, you catch my drift boy?"

"Well..."

"Don't you get smart with me, boy. And don't answer back." His eyebrows rise and fall, one higher than the other. "You take this as your final warning. I catch you one more time, I'm going to haul your tiny little Scottish arse in, you got me?" I nod. His hairy ears glow red. I can see those dobbers in the panel van and I think about how I'm going to pour sugar in their tank. He lets go. He tries to leave but realises the door opens inward and has to lean back into me so I lean back over the dunny and he gives me one more stare.

I straighten out my shirt, take a deep breath, weave through the crowds and go outside. I'm steaming.

Light reflects off the roof, with a touch of dew. The car park is full but there's no one around. Where did they all go? The panel van is gone. The cops are gone. My throat hurts from Taylor jamming his fist. I circle the lot a few times planning my revenge when I spot Terry's station wagon. I check to see if he's left his keys on top of the rear wheel but no luck. I use my pocket knife and force the driver's door open and start the car. I leave the lights off until I get out onto the road and drive north. They'll be at the Snake Pit and I'll flatten them for good.

In the heath there's no streetlights, just the odd house light. The road goes inland and follows the train line for a bit. I start to calm a little and wonder what I'm doing with Terry's car, and without Terry. He'd love a bit of biffo. I wind the window down and turn on the radio. Rabbits run into the bushes. I turn into a street lined with pine trees when the car starts spluttering and clunking and jerking against the accelerator. No petrol. The gauge doesn't work but I tap the screen anyway. I pull over so the car's half on the road, half off. The inside light is only just bright enough to shine in the back. I dig out a jerry can. Wrapped around the handle is a garden hose. I've got no money, and all the stations are shut, so I'll siphon some.

On a sandy verge is a Volkswagen Beetle. I open the wobbly front bonnet, unscrew the cap, feed the hose in and start sucking until the sweet burning hits my tongue and then shove the end in the jerry can. I pull the hose above the liquid to hear how much has gone in. Over the rise an engine rumbles and moves up through the gears, the glow of headlights too bright to make out the kind of car. I close the bonnet and take cover behind the bulging mudguards. The car drives up and stops behind the Beetle. A floodlight throws a shadow of the car onto the house. Out comes a Jack Russell yapping and yapping, running to and fro. On the house, a shadow of a man. My hands grip the bumper. Time to run. I spring to go but trip on a leg and then I'm pulled up onto the bonnet of the car.

"I told you to stay out of trouble Ronald. I told you back in the toilets if I caught you one more time I was going to take you in. Didn't I?" yells Taylor. The other cop shines his torch right in my eyes. The dog is yapping like crazy, setting off more dogs. Feels like everyone in the neighbourhood is coming to watch. "He's a stupid little bastard, this one," says Taylor.

"What you say his name was?" the other cop asks in an Irish accent.

"Ronald."

"I recognise him. Burnside and I questioned him last week, said his name was Warren."

"Thinks he's a smart arse. We got him for stealing petrol, lying to the police, and unlawful carnal knowledge."

"Carnal knowledge?" I ask.

"Shut the fuck up," he says. "You can start by putting the petrol back in the tank and then you can spend the night with us at the station." While I'm funneling the petrol back they stand around daring me to run off. The dog doesn't stop barking once. I look up at the moon.

The paddy wagon has two strips of dark blue vinyl padding running either side. The vinyl is cracked and the inner foam lets out a dead smell when you sit, like a million rotting rats. I lay my head back and feel the car idling. Fumes fill the wagon. I close my eyes and see Mum's face saying, *Told you so,* when Taylor rips through a turn throwing me across the wagon, nearly breaking my wrist.

"Sorry, Warren, forgot you were in there," says Taylor. They laugh to one another, a pair of galahs.

First thing I smell when I wake up is bleach, piss, and men's body odour. The metal framed bed has a thin mattress and blanket. I kick the blanket off and sit up. My shoes are gone, my jeans are ripped. My knuckles have scrapes and scabs. The song on the radio travels thin and tinny through the station. The walls are brick and painted cream colour. High up, there's a tight grilled screen inside a fibreglass window. A tiny slit to let in air. My ears burn, my ear drums ring.

The door has a little sliding flap. *Psst,* I hear. Just the bed springs bouncing. *Psst,* again. I shake my head. "Bon, Bon, you in there?" I look up, a black blob, Terry's head sideways, his lips in the air gap.

"Terry, where am I?"

"Freo station."

"Did you find your car?"

"Nah, where did you leave it?"

"In Swanbourne, near the tennis courts."

"Did you get 'em Bon? You break 'em in half? I wish I was there. Why didn't you come get me, coulda smashed them together."

"Your car ran out of petrol."

"If you had of come got me, I could have told you that."

"How'd you know I was in here?"

"Wild guess," says Terry.

"Don't tell anyone. I mean it, Terry. Not my brothers, Betty, no one." A big lump grows in my throat like I'm gunna cry. Outside I hear, *Oi, you, get away from that window, come here.* The thud of Terry's feet and him bolting. *Little bastard.* My head in my hands. Breathing in, breathing out. A tiny whistle on each inhale. Can't get air.

Next door a toilet flushes. A clanging in the locks. Taylor enters with a cup of water and some porridge. He sits his fat arse on the bed next to me. *Morning ,Ronald.* Hairs poke out of his fat nose. A forest of hair on top of his nose as well. He says I'll be in here another hour and then off to magistrate's court for a hearing. Pretends to be nice. Says his brother works with my dad. Everyone knows everyone around here. Whole town will know soon. Be in tomorrow's paper. Then Taylor changes his tune. He says he'll drop all the charges if I apologise and keep out of trouble. He says he sees ten kids like me come in each week. Says he loses his head from time to time.

He warns me they've built a juvenile detention centre out in woop woop and they're keen to fill it.

I tell him to stick it where the sun doesn't shine. They can give me everything they've got. He lets me go and says I'm due at the magistrate's court in an hour. Says if I don't turn up, they'll double the punishment.

It's a bright sunny day with no wind. Still early and the streets are quiet. I walk around by the parking lot, the department store, under the big figs, through the Freo mall, the bakery smell, the coffee and towards the post office. After walking around like this for ages I finally get to where I think the court is but it isn't. Turns out it's the town hall. I ask this man in a cape with a wig on, a judge or some lawyer type.

"Excuse me," I ask, trying to be all polite, "do you know where the magistrate's court is?" He's smoking a fag and he's walking so fast by the time I've finished asking he's a few yards ahead of me.

"Magistrate's court, hey old son?" He's got a big nose and huge eyebrows. His suit is black and he wears a black tie. He puts his fag in his lips, shifts his papers to one arm to free up his pointing arm. "See that street there? Well, that's fucking High Street." He's mumbling a bit on account of his fag. "Ya fucking take that street all the way to the fucking railway line. Once you hit the railway line go through the railway station. On the other side of the station is the port. On the other side of the port, pass the fucking art gallery and straight ahead is the court. Can't miss the cunt." By now I'm smiling my face off. He's talking so fast. He frowns at me and looks up the street the way he was heading before I stopped him. "You got that kiddo?" he asks, stamping out his fag, drawing attention to his fancy shoes.

"Got it," I say.

In the waiting room there's about a hundred people, mainly drunk sailors and locals with black eyes. We sit on long wooden benches, like church pews, and every five minutes an officer calls out someone's name. The ceiling is real high with beams jutting down. On the wall a coat of arms, a kangaroo and emu grazing. I wipe my sweaty palms on my dirty jeans. A cop goes in with most people. A couple of times just the cop goes in. I see a kid about my age come out, all sad. This makes my leg start jumping and I can't sit still.

My name gets called and I get up and go into a smaller room that doesn't look like a court room, just a few tables and chairs and a bar that the magistrate sits behind, reading. In walks cuntsable Taylor all clean shaven and straight faced, acting like he's never seen me before, saying, *yes your honour* this, *yes your honour* that, licking brown and so forth. The magistrate says I have three minutes, and judging by my case, since I'm a juvi, they want to keep the system freed up, he'll offer up an arrangement with Mum and Dad.

Next thing Taylor says his piece and he's getting to the bit about the petrol, lying through his teeth, and in walks me old mate with the wig, the one who was swearing his face off on the street. He puts some papers on the magistrates desk and walks out. The sight of him makes me smile. Then the magistrate slams his hand on the bench.

"Do you find this amusing, Master Scott?"

"Oh, no, sorry, your honour."

"Have you listened to a word I've said?"

"Yes."

"How old was the girl you allegedly had unlawful carnal knowledge with on the night in question?"

"Same age as all the other girls I've been with, I don't ask them how old they are. I'm lucky if they give me the time of day." There's a long silence as the magistrate reads through the papers.

"How do you plead to the charges, Mr Scott?" I don't care. What's the worst they can do?

"Guilty."

"As a juvenile I'm obliged by law to offer you to the custody of your parents. Although it's clear to me your parents don't have the ability to control you. Where are his parents?" he asks the woman at the desk. She says they've been informed and are on their way.

"Good," the magistrate says, peering over his glasses. "Master Scott, you have a choice. You either go home to your parents, attend school every day, or get a job. You will report to a parole officer every week, and we track your progress. Or, you spend time in juvenile detention for the crimes committed."

"I'll do the time," I say.

"I'm not sure you realise the gravity of the situation you're in, Master Scott."

"I'll do the time," I say. My leg bouncing like a pogo stick.

"In that case, I sentence you to nine months in Riverbank Detention Centre, with the possibility of weekend visits after three months. *Next.*" His gavel falls. I'm taken outside by one of the orderlies. I don't look at Taylor.

Mum is in the waiting room. She's carrying on saying, *Oh Ron.* When I tell her I got nine months she bursts out in tears. Then she catches herself and wipes her eyes with a handkerchief. The orderly says I can wait an hour for an escort or Mum can drive me. I don't have a choice. We jump in the Mini and pull out from behind a trolleybus and go uphill near the Dingo Flour Mill where you can look out over the railway tracks to the ocean and Rottnest. The wind bashes our car. Mum stutters up the gears, tucking her hair behind her ear, gripping the knob, blues veins in her white hands. Her blonde hair whips about behind her. I want to wrap my hand over hers and change gears together, like we used to.

We get clear of Stirling Highway and get a run on, driving by the university where Mum is a cleaner with the brown river to our right, green cliffs to our left. A pelican rocks in ferry waves. People are fishing. I wind the window down. Mum looks at me, serious, disappointed. We sit in silence for ages. I turn the radio on. Mum turns it up and starts singing. She has a good voice and knows all the words. She sings with the Scottish club every week. She always jokes about how she's going on tour with them, how Dad and us boys will have to look after ourselves. We follow the river for about an hour, crisscrossing bridges, going right up to a part I've never been before, real pretty bits you could camp and play in. Mum has to pull over to check the road book. We don't speak.

Up a gravel road with vineyards all around, a barking dog chasing us, we stop at the end of a fence. We approach a big iron gate and tall wire fences with barbed wire across the top. Everything looks like a farm, boys in blue overalls work in a vegie patch. We park between some gum trees. Mum sighs. To our left the big prison. Inside is a second set of fences, taller. We go into the red brick office building, and I have to say goodbye to Mum here and she starts crying and that makes me cry too. "Come home tae me my bonnie loon," she says, "come home to me."

There's a door next to the front counter, and I sign in and enter and to my surprise the people are friendly and I start to feel relieved. The fighting is over. A doctor checks me out and they give me a haircut and make me take a shower, and give me some overalls. They ask if I know anyone here and I say no. My cell is about three quarters the way down a long dark corridor. The walls are solid, there are no bars. Inside there are two beds, and someone's things are scattered all about. There's a fold up wooden table and wooden book shelves. There's a metal toilet, a basin and a towel rack.

A big guard comes along, throws some boots on the ground, grunts for me to put them on. He waits in the doorway. I say hello, but he doesn't reply. I look up and he says not to look at him. Boots on, he marches me to the sign in desk in the corner of the courtyard. This is where our movements are monitored. If you're in metalwork class and want to chuck a piss, you have to sign in first, and get a toilet pass. After the toilet, you sign out and go back to where you were. *No pass, no privileges.*

The guard shoves me in the back and takes me out to the vegie patch and I pick up a shovel and start digging. There's about twenty of us. No one is talking. Pretty soon I have my overalls tied around my waist like everyone else. They make us pick all the worms off the leaves and throw them in a bucket. My back is sore. Silence. No singing, no talking. Songs going round and round inside my head. Crows in the trees. One kid, Norman, who is my cell-mate, watches the crows carefully.

Every day at 6:42am and 9:25pm an airplane crosses our cell window. You can hear other planes during the day, but these you can see. They're like little white toys against a blue sky, with a red tail. The window is four hands wide and four hands high. The bars are oval shaped, welded at the tips. On the outside is a grille. Over the grille a fly wire full of holes. The holes let the mosquitoes in, but not out. In the evening they start their buzzing. In the morning I wake up and my feet and face are pocked with bites. Norman says rubbing piss on them stops the itching.

At night we slap ourselves silly killing mozzies. One night we caught over a hundred. To catch them in the dark the trick is to cover your whole body with a blanket, and leave a little opening over your mouth. Norman reckons they're attracted to your breath. When they're above your face you clap them dead. We catch them until we fall asleep. When I wake up my bed and the ground is covered in little black spots. I pick up a few and pull them apart. Snap their bodies in half. Let the blood ooze out. We brush them up into a pile.

Lights out at nine and then the 9:25 plane. You can hear the engines revving up before take off. I hear songs in the build up. A loud rock band shaking your bones, taking away your blues. Norman is quiet. He's tall and wiry. He avoids eye contact when you speak to him. We share comic strips and talk about them after.

Nine full moons. Nine full moons and I'm free. Most others have a calendar they cross off everyday. I have an outline of nine moons drawn on the wall. I draw in each phase, filling it up every few days. Norman says the moons look beautiful. I ask him what he knows about beauty. He says I better watch it or he'll pick out the beauty on my face and put it elsewhere. He's quick. His cheeks bunch up, as if someone stuck some golf balls in his mouth. Next thing we're wrestling on the floor with the dead mozzies and stinking boots. He's stronger than me even though he's more wiry. He says when the Southern Cross is on the horizon it's time to go hunting for emu eggs. He says he and his brothers used to live in the bush. They used to chop off all the saplings after the bulldozers took out the trees with a chain between them.

Six times a day you hear the bell go off over at Govo, the high school across the river. Then you hear the screaming and laughing and flirting. I imagine I can fly out the window and play with the girls. I need love real bad. Man, you don't even have to do anything with the girls but be in their company, smell their hair.

Same river leads back to my house. Same river they let us swim in once when the weather got real hot. Swinging upside down on a rope tied to a branch. Reckon I could swim home in a few hours. Norman says to swim to North Freo would take two days. Says you'd have to sleep under bridges and steal food. Maybe I will when they let me out. Run across the paddock and dive in and swim back. Feel the cool water. Find parts of the river no one has seen before. Other side of the Narrows I know pretty well, where the water turns from brown to blue. Swim to Pelican Point, then to Point Walter, then to Black Wall Reach and then I'm home, dripping wet on Mum's door step.

HI SUZY,

PLEASE WRITE MORE AS I REALLY LIKE TO HEAR FROM YOU.

DON'T WORRY ABOUT UPSETTING ME BY TALKING ABOUT WHAT'S GOING ON OUTSIDE. IN HERE YOU HAVE TO ENJOY THE LITTLE THINGS. I HAVE ~~LEARNED~~ LEARNT TO SHAVE. I SHAVE ONE SIDE AT A TIME, A RITUAL I GO THROUGH.

ONCE A WEEK THIS OLD DUCK COMES IN TO READ POETRY TO US. WAS EITHER THAT OR SIT IN MY CELL. SHE READ THE RHYME OF THE ANCIENT MARINER. YOU READ IT? ALL THEIR FACES CRACKED AND THE OLD MAN LEFT ALONE ON THE SHIP. ONE DAY SHE GOT US TO WRITE OUR OWN STUFF. HERE'S WHAT I WROTE:

LET ME IN YOUR HOUSE
WHEN YOUR PARENTS ARE ASLEEP
I'M NOT YOUR LOVER
LET ME SHOW YOU MY LOVE

I'VE BEEN BAD FOR MOST OF MY LIFE
YOU'LL SEE MY FACE BELOW THE BRIDGE
LET MY INTO YOUR HOUSE
LET ME SHOW YOU MY LOVE

LET ME SHOW YOU MY LOVE
LET ME SHOW YOU THE SCENE
LET ME SHOW YOU MY LOVE
LIKE IT'S A NIGHTMARE OR A DREAM

WHAT DO YOU THINK? ONE THING I DID LEARN IS THAT MY WRITING ALWAYS COMES OUT LIKE SONG LYRICS. I CAN'T SEPARATE THE MUSIC FROM THE WORDS. LAST WEEK THE OLD DUCK READ US SOME POEMS BY A GUY NAMED ELIOT. I COULDN'T HEAR THE MUSIC. THE IMAGERY WAS GOOD BUT NO MUSIC. SHE SAYS I HAVE A TALENT FOR MUSIC AND LYRICS. ONE MINUTE I FEEL ON TOP OF THE WORLD EVERY WORD COMING OUT EASY, AND THEN THE NEXT MINUTE I'M SO LONELY AND MISS EVERYONE AND I WANT TO KNOW WHAT ALL THIS MESS IS ABOUT.

TAKE CARE,

BON.

Friday, Norman and my turn to scrub the toilet block. The big guard we call Monkey waits for us after breakfast. We get given a bucket each, with a brush, a squirt of bleach and some hot water. The block has concrete floors and green tiled walls. There's steel basins and tiled showers. A gully runs between the showers. A piss trough and five shitters. There's a locked cupboard with soap and towels. Signs everywhere telling you what to do. *Throw your discarded soap in the bins please.*

Norman and I start cleaning one end and work our way to the other. We're on our hands and knees and I can hardly breathe. Monkey doesn't let us chat. I can't see his face. All I see are his black boots. We've been scrubbing for about an hour, half the job done. I look up and ask for a glass of water.

"Drink the water in the bucket," says Monkey. I stand up and stretch my back and go to drink from the basin tap and get a head-spin. A tingling in my hands and feet. Monkey puts his hand on my shoulder and forces me to the ground and I try to start scrubbing, my hand shaking and I tell Norman I'm going to have an asthma attack and Norman tells Monkey I need my puffer real quick.

"I not stupid," Monkey says. "You play trick to get out of work, you finish the scrub, you have your puffer." He kicks the bucket and dirty water flops on the floor and he says, "Hurry up or I make you fight each other." I can't get any air in. I try to cough but take a mouthful of bleach fumes and feel sick. I try to talk but can't. I go to stand to walk outside but Monkey pushes me to the wet floor and Norman yells, "He's going to pass out, can't you hear him wheezing?" The green tiles blur. Norman runs and screams for help and Monkey chases after him and I'm breathing though a tiny straw that's shrinking. I close my eyes.

I wake on the grass with the sun in my face, some kind of breathing device in my mouth. They take me to the nurse's station on a stretcher and they ask if I want to ring my mother but I say no, take me to my cell. Taking a suck of my puffer every so often I read through all my letters and postcards. I get to thinking everyone sounds so sad and bored on the outside. Maybe they don't want to make it sound like they're having too much fun cause they don't want to make me sad, but I couldn't get much sadder.

Pull the pillow over my head and get so angry and feel like I have no control and hate Monkey and how he has control and I have none. I punch and kick the bed and pillow. Norman comes in says I better slow down or I'll have another asthma attack. He lays crossways on the bed with his feet up on the wall. He's quiet and still and reads a comic. He giggles every now and then. Then he asks me if I want to hear a joke and I say no.

"A horse walks into a bar," he says. "Barman says, why the long face?"

"Not now, Norman. I'm not in the mood."

"You cry enough to water a camel. You given up, huh?" asks Norman. "You wanna hide under that blanket forever?" I don't answer. A couple of minutes later he farts. "You know they say jail changes a man?" His voice is getting all excited.

"Oh yeah?" I say.

"Yeah, I used to be white." His feet start pattering on the wall. His calf muscles wobble, the room fills with his laughter.

"I'm gunna get him," I say. He pushes his feet off the wall and we square off. "One day I'm gunna get that Monkey bastard, *get him good.*" My shoulders and lips tense.

"Oh, you the man, hey Ronald? Big *king dick.* Bet you got it all figured out. Only thing you got figured is out is how to be miserable. I tell you what. You're not going to do nothing.

You're never going to win. Like punching a wall of sand, those fellas."

"Oh yeah, what makes you the expert?"

"Sixteen years they give me. I'll be thirty when I'm out. I stabbed one of 'em."

"Jesus Christ, Norman. What happened?"

"Off season, they's picking on my dad, in Toohey's Gardens, you know it?" His eyebrows poke out, creases in his forehead, a lump between his eyes bolted with blood.

"No."

"Don't matter. You're not gunna stay stuck in here. No, you gotta jump for one of those planes and shoot for the sky, unna?"

"Hey?"

"Understand?"

"What about you?"

"What about me?"

"What are you gunna do?"

"There's a Nyoongar trick I'm trying to learn. Turn into a crow and fly off." He holds his palm out and slowly brings it to my face. I go with him. Some kind of ritual. Gets to be his right hand in my face and I can smell the bleach, see the lines in his palm, his white teeth showing. Then he slaps me real hard on the forehead and jumps back on his bed and starts laughing.

"What'd you do that for?"

"Mozzie," he says, and shows me the blood on his fingers.

"How long you got left in here, Bon?"

"Two months?"

"What are you gunna do when you get out?"

"Join a band."

"Oh yeah, you gunna rule the world, like Elvis, or the Beatles?"

"Maybe not Elvis, more like Chuck Berry, the master."

"Go on then Chuck, sing us a number."

"What? Now?"

"You not gunna sing now, when are you gunna sing?" Then he starts singing.

EVERYDAY IT'S GROWING BETTER
GOIN FASTER THAN A DIRT RACER
LIFE LIKE THIS WILL SWING MY WAY
MAY-HEY-BE

I join in.

EVERYDAY I'M IN THIS PLASTER
WARDEN SAYS WE'RE NOWHERE AFTER
LIFE LIKE THIS WILL SWING MY WAY
MAY-HEY-BE

I open my eyes. He's sitting cross legged, clapping, bouncing on the mattress. From the next cell they're yelling, "Eh you two lover birds, give it a rest, you sing like dying dingoes."

"It's hard without instruments," I say.

"Gotta listen for your own rhythm," he says, his voice a little dry. I stand up and start dancing. My stomach expands and contracts. I clench my toes and focus on the sound. I close my eyes and see the crowd at the Port Beach stomp, all their faces. I make words up.

MUM AND DAD WERE OUT AT WORK
MY BROTHERS WERE OUT AT SCHOOL
THEY LEFT ME HOME ALONE
SINGING AND PLAYING THE FOOL

When I open my eyes I'm not facing the way I thought I'd be. Norman is lying on his bed, blanket pulled up. His eye lids squint, his lashes all clustered. I lie down as well. The lights go out.

"Got that footy match in the afternoon," he says. He's a gun

player. "You gunna play this time?"
"Alright," I say, "you boys need a win."

THE VALENTINES
Melbourne — 1969

I get up and chuck a shit. Earliest bird gets the freshest air. The valve is broken in the cistern, and water drips onto the back of the bowl, making a brown line. Everyone is still in bed, except Darc, who's gone to get the paper, milk and bread. He's our roadie and there's no stopping the bastard. I stare at the back of the door.

When I arrived at Suzy's her parents were starting lunch. Through the sliding door I could see the table set, some of the nosh spread out. I knocked on the door and Suzy answered and she gave me a big hug. As soon as her father saw me he left the dining room and went and sat in the lounge room. He was banging on the T.V. trying to make it work. He had no chin and his hair was combed. Suzy had warned me he was strict. Her mother had to take his lunch into him. We ate. I tried to be as polite as possible and thanked Suzy's mum for the food. Eventually he gave up and turned the T.V. off and sat by himself. I grabbed two beers from the fridge and offered him one.

"How are you, Mister Van Dyke?" I said, leaning on the door frame.

"Good," he said, moving back in his seat.

"My dad tells me you're keeping well."

"Mm."

"Would you like a beer, Mister Van Dyke?"

"No."

DEAR SUZY,

HOW ARE YOU TWEETY? HOW IS PERTH? STILL WINDY? ARE YOU COMING TO MELBOURNE SOON? SORRY ABOUT WHAT HAPPENED WITH JOHN FARNHAM THAT NIGHT. I GOT CARRIED AWAY AND DRANK TOO MUCH, AS USUAL. NOT MUCH I CAN SAY ABOUT THAT OTHER THAN I'M A FUCK UP.

SCORED THIS FLAT ON DALGETY ST IN ST. KILDA. IT'S GOOD OTHER THAN THE ROOF LEAKS AND THE CATS PISS EVERYWHERE.

LAST WEEK WE DID A COCA-COLA COMMERCIAL AND TWO WEEKS BEFORE THAT WE DROVE UP TO SYDNEY, NEWCASTLE AND BRISBANE. SLEEPING ON MATTRESSES ON TOP OF THE GEAR IN THE VAN.

ANYWAY THE REASON WHY I AM WRITING IS BECAUSE I THINK WE SHOULD MAYBE BE WITH OTHER PEOPLE, DON'T YOU? WE HAD A GOOD HOT GO, BUT WE DON'T SEEM TO BE ABLE TO GET IT TOGETHER. ON THE PHONE YOU SAID YOU DIDN'T TRUST ME. I HAVEN'T BEEN WITH ANYONE ELSE FOR AGES. I MISS OUR DAYS IN EAST FREO WHEN IT WAS ONLY ME AND YOU AND THE RADIO AND OUR TOASTED EGG SANDWICHES.

HOPE YOU GET THIS BEFORE YOU BOOK YOUR TICKET. I'M GOING TO BE AWAY THAT WEEKEND.

LOTS OF LOVE,
BON.

On the outside of the envelope I write a message to her father: *OPEN THIS AND I'LL PUNCH YOUR LIGHTS OUT.*

I put the kettle on. Soon after, Gabby, Darc's girlfriend, walks in, dressed for work.

"Morning, Bon," she says, starting to make eggs.

"What are you guys doing today?"

"Same thing we do every day, rehearsing then playing tonight."

"That's not what I meant, smartypants." There are yawns and groans from the lounge room. Egg whites flap in the pan. Seven of us in this two bedroom flat. There's Darc, our roadie. Gabby. Wyn, our guitarist. Ted, the bass player, and Paddy, on drums. Lastly, there's Vince, the other singer. He stayed somewhere else last night. Every morning we pack the mattresses away and practice. Then in the afternoon we get our costumes ready and head out for an afternoon show, have a break and then a night show.

Darc walks in looking like someone kicked him in the balls, his eyes all watery. He's wearing white sand shoes, jeans and a blue sports jacket. He throws the shopping on the floor.

"Darc, what's the matter?" asks Gabby.

"My number's up," he says. He's a little fella, smaller than me.

"Your what?"

"Twelve, number twelve. I've got the call up," he says.

"Show me," Gabby grabs the letter out of his hand. I pull a chair out for him. *In my mind I see Dad and me in the Mini. The Swanbourne barracks. Two rows of fibro buildings, stained with bore water. An army office.*

"This is bullshit," Gabby says, snapping me out of my daydream. Her neck extends.

"You can get out of it mate," I tell him.

"How?"

"Fail the test," says Gabby.

"Be useless," I say.

"He's already an expert at that Bon," says Gab, chuffed with her own joke.

"I'm serious," I say. "I had a test in Perth about three years ago, after Riverbank. My parole officer made me. All you have to do is fake a permanent injury, or pretend to be a homo."

"Fair dinkum?" Darc looks at me hopeful.

"They said I was socially maladjusted."

"They were right about that," says Darc, smiling, a gap in his two front teeth. "I *could* go to jail." He's slumped in his chair, as if he's about to fall off it. Gabby has to go to work. She kisses him on the forehead, grabs her bag, and goes. I take out the mull tin from the second drawer and hand it to Darc and start making tea and eggs for the both of us. He re-reads the letter.

"Fuck 'em," he says, grimacing, crows feet around his eyes. "I'll go bush. Stupid fucking war. These pricks at the top never get sick of it. If people come and invade us, we'll just drop our things and go, but to be plucking guys who are twenty years old, in the prime of their lives." He waves his fork around.

"It's been good knowing ya," I say, taking a toke.

"You cheeky bastard." There's a knock at the door. Probably Vicki, our next door neighbour. She's a bit loopy, and from Adelaide. The groupies aren't due for another few hours. "You making cookies?" he asks.

"You burned them last time," I say.

"Still got us stoned." I pull the dough out of the fridge. More knocking at the door.

"Answer the door, Bon," he says, sucking on the roach.

"You answer the door. Why should I answer the door?"

"I got the ballot, mate. I'm off to Nui Dat. They're gunna blow me away." He sticks out his lower lip. Ted and Wyn and Paddy are awake, lying in their blankets. Bloke smell. I push the window curtain with the back of my hand. A brunette wearing glasses and freckles fidgets at the door. Wet footmarks on the concrete path. Under her arm two long plastic tubes.

"I'm an arts student at Melbourne Uni." She asks, "do you want to buy one of my paintings?"

"We don't have any money," I tell her. I imagine her naked. She has wide, farm girl hips, large nipple pads. She is looking past me into the loungeroom.

"I don't have any money either, that's why I'm selling my paintings cheap. Come on, you must have five dollars or so." She is desperate, but not for sex. Neighbours watch from their balconies.

"What's that smell?" she asks.

"Cookies," I say.

She barges by me and into the kitchen. The boys are cleaning up. I go into the bathroom and brush my teeth and hair. When I finish Ted is shining his shoes, Wyn is tuning his guitar and Paddy is eating a bowl of cereal. In the kitchen, the girl is pulling her paintings from the tubes and laying them on the floor. Darc flings a tea towel over his shoulder and raises his eyebrows.

"Last night's show," says Ted, not looking up from his red boots. "Too much Vince. You have to sing more, Bon, he's killing us." Wyn looks up briefly, winding the machine head on his guitar.

"Vince does all the organising and promotion, Ted. We've talked about this before. We'd be stuffed without him. You wanna go schmooze with all those Melbourne wankers?" I say. Darc opens the oven door and checks the cookies.

"I'm not talking about kicking him out of the band. Just changing the direction of the music a bit. More Jethro and Santana and Stones stuff instead of this nick-nack-paddy-whack rubbish." Wyn's finished tuning and starts warming up. Darc takes the cookies out and takes to them with the egg flip. The earthy mull smell is strong. The girl starts eating, blowing the steam off. Darc and I smirk.

"Why did you sit there?" he asks me.

"What are you talking about?"

"I mean, out of all the places in the flat to sit, you sat there, how come?" His little eyes are bloodshot. A Hank Williams record comes on from the living room.

"I felt like it, Darc."

"What do you call that one, Charmaine?" Darc asks the girl. "The one that looks like a jockey riding an elephant in the jungle."

"Looks more like a bird in a spaceship to me," I say.

"It's me riding a unicorn," she says, sipping a glass of milk.

"Oh."

"Oh, yeah, now I see it, you look different," says Darc, enjoying this game.

"What about that one?" says Ted, pointing.

"That's definitely a purple waterfall falling into a pool of yellow sand," I say.

Adds Darc, "I reckon it's a big gum tree that's been eating too many plums." She looks up at us, her eyes glazing over.

"Or a jacaranda with the flowers falling," joins in Wyn.

"Some kind of tree, isn't it?" asks Ted. The front door opens and Vince walks in, he's got bell bottoms and a purple sweater on.

"What have we got here then, sweetheart?" he moves in. She shakes him off. He sees the tray with the mull cookies, picks one up and starts eating. "So yous've been getting stoned while I've been out booking shows?" Crumbs fly from his mouth, he waves the biscuit about. "Guess where we've got a week long residency starting on Friday?"

"Where?" asks Ted.

"Jan Juc," says Vince, excited.

"Jan Juc?" says Wyn, playing his guitar.

"Jan Juc? You've got to be joking," says Ted.

"Where the fuck is Jan Juc?" I ask.

"Some surf town near Torquay," says Darc, watching Charmaine. She's on her tip toes, looking out the window.

"Where's Torquay?" I ask.

"Near Geelong. Jesus, Bon, don't you know anything?" says Vince.

"Not as much as you, Vince," says Ted.

"*Jan Juc, Jan Juc, where the fuck is Jan Juc*," I sing.

"I thought we were working toward going to England?" asks Wyn.

"Here we go, me against the rest of you again," says Vince. He looks like a turtle when he gets angry. Ted and Vince have been at each other for weeks. "I'm out there talking to dozens of people trying to get us gigs, and I have to come back to this shit?"

"Every time I put a show together you take over anyway," says Ted, crossing his arms.

"Calm down everyone," says Wyn.

"Nah, fuck him." Ted stands up, "We all work as hard as each other, don't come barging in complaining we never do anything." Charmaine stands at the sink, arms locked straight, palms flat against the metal. She stares into the sink. Then paces the kitchen. We look at each other confused. She looks up into the window.

"Mechanical flying kangaroos," she says.

"Ahhh," says Darc, clapping his hands, looking back at the canvas, "I never would have guessed that. You see the roos, Bon?"

"She's not talking about the painting Darc, I think she's hallucinating. How many cookies did she eat?"

"A couple," Darc says, shrugging.

"Feel like getting some fresh air, Charmaine?"

"I've got two sisters and a brother, my uncle has a beach house in Jan Juc" she says, her hair all messy, looking a bit sick.

"I never said that," says Vince. "Bonnie boy, back me up, you know how hard it is to get a residency."

"I love Jan Juc," says Charmaine, "my parents have a holiday home there." She looks terrible.

"You boys got her *real* fucked up," says Vince.

"My dad, he's a cop, he kicked me out," she says, her eyes rolling in their sockets.

"Come on, darling, let's take you home," says Darc, picking up the paintings.

"Who's got some money for one of her paintings?" I ask.

"What for? They're terrible," says Ted.

"Who cares what they look like, we've got to get rid of her," says Darc. Ted and Wyn pull out some coins and lay them on the table. Darc and I start to carry her out to the van. There's a few groupies waiting by the brick letterboxes out front. The neighbours are watching us.

"They're gunna think we drugged and raped her," I say.

"I was thinking the same thing," says Darc, clutching one of the tubes under his armpit.

"Stand her up."

"Stand up, Charmaine, that's a girl." The apartments are long and face the road. Stairwells break the buildings up. Out the back is the car park and a grassed area with clotheslines. We get her onto the passenger seat of the Kombi. Darc's little body jumps up and down pumping the accelerator. "You coming?" he asks.

"Nah, this'll be good training for you," I say. "Ambulance driver in the army." There's a thud on my upper arm.

"Watchya doin', Bon?" It's Vicki, our neighbour. She goes to grab my balls. I pull back.

"Stop it," I say. Darc revs the engine, and begins to reverse.

"Charmaine," Vicki yells, her voice is deep and booming.

"*Keep quiet,*" I say.

"What for?" Vicki asks. When Darc stops she stands at the door and taps the window. "Charmaine," she says again. Darc leans over and winds the window down.

"You know her?" Charmaine's head flops from one side to the other.

"Yeah," she says, "know her from Adelaide." Darc revs the engine and drives the Kombi back to its first spot. He gets out and picks Charmaine up, tells me to grab the tubes.

"She's staying with you, Vicki," he says. "Open your door."

In the car park behind the apartments, Darc has his head buried in the engine bay at the back of the Kombi. He's going to drop us off in Jan Juc then drive back, because he has the army medical on Monday. Ted, Wyn, Paddy and I pile all the gear in the car park. Darc has to pack it in a special order. While he's doing that we buy some flash bombs and I fire off my letter to Suzy. I go to the chemist and get some extra asthma puffers. When I get back Darc is jamming some mattresses on top of the gear. Vince arrives in a station wagon.

"Whose is that?" I ask him.

"Borrowed it, mate," he says, poking his tongue out.

"Nice of you to let us know," says Darc, "Could've packed differently. The other boys can go with you then."

"I'll pick up the P.A. as well," says Vince.

"You can get the weed too," I tell him.

"No worries, mate," he says, putting his arm on the door frame.

"You wearing that?" he asks, nodding at me. I'm wearing denim shorts and a singlet.

"Yeah, what's wrong with this?"

"Got your new costumes?"

"They're upstairs." He drives away and I go upstairs and start packing my clothes, puffy shirts and flared women's pants. Fuck him, I'm not wearing this shit anymore. Darc barges in and says he needs a hand, push-starting the van. We pull out onto Dalgety Street in the shade of the figs. We head out of the city, the factories thinning out.

The train slowed on the outskirts of Melbourne. Through the factories we moved. I watched out for the station names. The windscreens of the cars were covered in frost. A man stood on his bonnet and pissed on his windscreen. He looked up and waved at the train. Spencer Street. The station was massive, almost five times bigger than Perth Station. Ten lines of tracks. Passengers were slowly waking and lowering their luggage from the overhead compartments. Ted still slept. Wyn woke him and stood up in the aisle. His usually combed hair was all frazzled and messy. Vince was organised and standing at the door with his bags. He winked. He had everything under control. We made it. Melbourne, at last. The doors opened. Cool air smacked our faces. I picked up my bags and Ted's bass. We all piled out and gathered on the platform. Vince held a small piece of white paper. It was Ronnie Burns' phone number.

On each side of the highway farmhouses and green paddocks. We stop in Geelong to buy food. "Don't let me forget thongs, Darc," I say. We pull open the glass doors. To our right more glass windows with sale posters. The high ceiling has lights hanging off them. Plastic chairs, bins, buckets, mops, irons, aprons, torches, flags, lollies, washing powder, washing boards, shampoo and all sorts of stuff. A girl at the counter, a bored looking blonde. We're the only customers. There are some novelty aprons with wombats on them and another set with fake boobs. I slip one on. Darc has found a pogo stick and starts bouncing along an aisle. The springs squeak. I wrap a feather boa around my neck, grab some egg flips and potato mashers and ask the girl where the thongs are. Without looking up from her magazine she says, "Middle of row five."

"You got the small rubber ones?" I ask. "I don't like the big cardboard ones." She looks up and I pout and she giggles. I strap some of the air fresheners shaped like little trees to my armpits and I ask her which scent she prefers. She says I better stop or I'll get her in trouble. *Aren't you looking for trouble?* She steps back, placing her hands on the pole behind her. Her breasts poke out. I like her freckles and crooked teeth. A bouncy ball flies from Darc's direction knocking over a stand of fly spray. I sing, *I'm Louie the fly, I'm Louie the fly, straight from rubbish tip to you.* I run around the counter performing for her, using the masher as a microphone.

"Where are you guys from?" she asks. I grab a few wigs and throw them in the air. Darc comes out holding some old ladies pink fluffy slippers.

"These what you're looking for, Bon?" I try them on, too small. I flick them in the air. She keeps pivoting on the pole watching us. I lean in and read her name badge. Julianne. I make up a song for her.

Julianne, with hair so strong, you stand there wrong, and mad.
Julianne, you can find your way, til next weeks pay, and glad.

Darc bounces by on the pogo stick, his Popeye forearms poking out. He holds a tambourine that jangles as he bounces. Julianne throws a boa at him and it gets caught in the springs and he goes flying into a stack of black plant pots. She and I laugh our heads off. Darc starts walking toward us like a martian with pots as hands. "I am Frank from Frankston, you will..." The office doors slams.

"It's my boss," says Julianne. Darc and I run up an aisle and hide.

"What's all this mess," he yells at her. He's dark haired and wears a cheap suit. She doesn't answer. He's bending over picking things up. "Julianne, answer me, this is the last time I will ask you." She starts weeping. "Every time I leave the store you screw up. You arrive late, you undercharge some people and overcharge others. I've nearly had my lot with you." I feel so bad. It's not her fault. I walk up to the front desk and tell him not to punish her, to leave her alone. He looks at me with the fake boobs and feather boas. He stares at my tattoos.

"You know this guy?" he asks her.

"No, he came in just now," she sobs. The manager threatens

to call the cops.

"No, no, no, no, we'll clean it all up," says Darc.

"How many are there?"

"Just me and him." We clean up and I find the thongs I need. "Lend me a few bob, will ya, Darc?"

As we enter the corners, the Kombi leans and the pale trunks of the paperbarks stick out beneath the green tops. Glimpses of the ocean. A small hawk hovers. A kangaroo runs out onto the road and Darc dodges it and keeps driving and the roo jumps beside us and then veers off into a gully. "*Suicidal little bastards,*" he says. The black knob is broken off the handle, but I manage to wind the window down and smell the sea salt and seaweed and the waft of bushes that smell like lavender mixed with whacky tobacky.

The surf club is similar to the one at Port Beach, but bigger. A two storey job, with roller doors on both sides of the building. Long boats and showers on the ground floor and upstairs glass windows all around. I walk straight to the beach. Over in the distance, great sandy cliffs all jagged like a cheese grater. A bloke walks along the bottom of the cliff with a board under his arm. I strip off and run into the freezing water, diving over the waves. I stand on a sand bar. I wipe my eyes and clear my nose and see Vince standing on the balcony, watching me. I feel him thinking about the band. I can forgive him the way the others can't. He's ambitious.

A large wave approaches and I duck dive through the face and emerge where I can't stand. I swim overarm for while until I feel a strange tingle on my arm. Stingers. When I return Darc has most of the gear upstairs. My arms and chest are covered in goosebumps and my nipples are erect. I ask the club manager for some vinegar and go into the kitchen and pour some on the stinger welts. Inside the walls are covered in photos and first place ribbons and dried out shark jaws. Vince is making some sandwiches.

"Nice of you to help us," he says.

"Guess we're sleeping on the floor," I say.

"Lucky I bought the mattresses," he says.

People start arriving around sunset. I grab a bourbon and Coke and go to sit on the balcony. Darc is running around like a maniac setting everything up. He has trouble getting the P.A. working. Lastly, he sets the flash bombs up and we're ready to go. Vince comes charging out, all dressed up.

"You getting ready?" he asks, heaving. His hair is all straightened and bobbed at the shoulders. "We're going on in ten minutes," he says. "Get ready, mate."

"I can't," I say, sucking on an ice block.

"Why not?"

"Don't have my costume."

"Oh, for fuck's sakes. Don't expect to sing any songs tonight," he says, and goes back inside. The wind bends the tops of the bushes, and they spring back.

"G'day," says a bloke, handing me a bourbon. A surfy guy with long red hair. "This is Keith, Johnny, and I'm Stuey," he says. We shake hands.

"I'm Bon, Bon Scott. You blokes live here?"

"Up the road," says Stuey. We keep chatting and I can see Darc running back and forward between the mixing desk and microphones. He looks over and indicates for me to get up. The band plays *Everyday I Have to Cry.* The place starts to fill up and some girls start dancing on the wooden floor near the stage. I'm starting to get a bit tipsy, but good tipsy. The song finishes and there's a break between songs while Wyn tunes up. Paddy fixes the position of his cymbal stands.

"Not a bad band," says Stuey.

"You reckon?" says Johnny. Wyn starts playing the opening riff from *Good Times Bad Times,* the new Led Zeppelin song. Ted waves me over. Paddy joins Wyn with his hi-hat. I walk as casually as possible to the stage and take the mike off the stand. The first verse has finished and I join Vince for the chorus. Darc lets some firebombs go off, smiling from ear to ear, and the girls start screaming and there's high-pitched whistles from the balcony. I give it everything, screaming my lungs out til I nearly fall over, the room spinning. We fade out like on the album, and the whole room erupts in applause. We launch into *Helter Skelter* straight away and the next two hours blast by, Stuey bringing me bourbons through the set. Wyn and Ted and Paddy playing great. By the time we finish I'm sweating like a pig.

At midnight the cops arrive and kick everyone out, turn the lights off and close the door. Ted and Wyn and Vince go outside and chat to everyone. A couple of girls come up to me looking for action and I tell them to hide behind the drum kit and I lay a blanket over them. Darc comes over, wearing a blue jacket.

"Thought you were going home," I say.

"Someone had to control the flash bombs," he says. "Anyway, someone had to turn Vince's microphone down. I'm glad I stuck around to see you, you crazy bastard." The manager turns all the lights off.

"You liked it, huh?"

"Mate, I've been telling you, fuck that bubblegum shit off."

"Come with me," I tell him. Everything feels sped up. In the dark I make my way to the girls and lift up the blanket. They've already taken their clothes off and I feel their cool firm skin. We pair off and work our way to the front of the drum kit and lie down. I kiss her and take a handful of bum. I slide my hand in from the back and work my fingers in, moist and warm. She groans softly. I undo my fly and pull my shorts halfway down my thighs. When I look up I see Darc's face in front of me and the top of his girls' head.

"You're a lucky bastard," he says. I kiss the girl's neck and she spreads her legs and slides my dick inside. She's tight so I go slow and it hurts a little. I bang my right knee on the floor.

I start to go faster and by the sound of his breathing, Darc is too. His small face wincing in pleasure, the gap in his teeth showing.

Outside I hear, "They won't be coming back anytime soon," and a jangling at the door then the door flies open throwing the streetlight on us. Even though my ears are ringing I hear the lights fire up, one flash, two flashes, then the lights on right above us. I don't dare to look, except at Darc, who's really going for it. The girl under him, her hair flayed out on the floor, plastic cups and a foldback speaker next to us. The girl under me looks over to the bar and starts lifting her pelvis more. "Come on," she says. The boys who have walked in all notice us and start cheering and yelling.

Darc lets out a kind of hiss and starts coming, his girl arching and grabbing his back, and he convulses and then collapses on her. I follow not long after, not really feeling like a proper climax. I pull out and roll over and put my shorts back on. The barman puts some music on and the drinking starts. I apologise to the girl, but she doesn't seem to care, she goes over to the bar and joins in. They're playing a drinking game called *Song of the Gooniebird*, like pass the parcel, but if the music stops you have to drink. The barman lets us have whatever we want. Darc drives back to St. Kilda.

Ted shakes me. My head feels like it's about to explode. There's a banging at the door. I'm lying on the floor, no mattress, no blanket. There's a light on behind the bar. Vince is asleep on his arms, slumped on a table. Wyn is walking towards the door. *BANG BANG BANG*. "Open the door, it's the police." Two blue uniforms barge in. My mouth is so dry. They start going through all of our stuff, looking inside the bass drum, the guitar cases, turning Wyn's acoustic upside down. Then I remember the weed in the back of the speaker box. I try to wake Vince but he raises his head like a long neck turtle, and falls back to sleep.

"You got a warrant?" I yell.

"This your place, is it?" the tall, skinny cop yells back, his face full of scorn. He starts poking his arm inside the bass cabinet and I know we're done for. Ted and Wyn sit at my table, their costumes stained. "Well, well, well," the cop says, holding up the bag. "What have we here?"

"I would say that's marijuana," the other cop says, taking a whiff. "Is this yours?" he asks Ted, who looks at me. The little one pulls out a note pad and starts scribbling. The big one runs out to the car and returns with some kitchen scales. Just under half an ounce. Three fingers. Seems no point in lying or trying to get out it. I give them our names and addresses. When they leave Ted and I pour ourselves a whisky and go back to sleep. The sun is rising.

I wake up at about noon, still drunk. Flashes of last night come to me as I lay among plastic cups, cigarette butts, streamers and empty bottles. Vince sits at one of the tables, smoking a cigarette, drinking a coffee. Wyn is outside on the balcony playing his guitar. Ted is behind the bar and offers to make me a coffee.

"Why didn't you wake me up?" asks Vince, the blue infringement papers on the table in front of him.

"Morning, Vince," I say, feeling like there's a knife in the back of my head.

"This is fucking serious, Bon. Why didn't you wake me up?"

"We tried, you were as dead as a door nail, asleep on the table there."

"I could've stopped them," he jabs his smoke out in an ashtray.

"There's nothing you could have done," says Ted, handing me a coffee. "They came in and started searching, they knew there was stuff here." He pushes his hand up into his face and drags his fingers over his eyebrows.

"So you expect me to take the fall for this?" says Vince. "I'm not taking responsibility for something I wasn't even awake for. Who gave them my name?" I watch the yellow bubbles circle in the coffee. "Who gave them my name?"

"It was all over in less than half an hour, wasn't it, Bon?" says Ted.

"Who. Gave. Them. My. Name?" His top lip curls. His fists clench. He looks me straight in the eye. I look him straight back and chuckle. I'd tear him apart and he knows it. I bring the coffee to my mouth and blow the steam off.

"You can't have it both ways, Vince," I tell him as he moves his seat back. "We tried to wake you up. We couldn't. So either we woke you up and you gave them your name yourself, or you were asleep, because you were too pissed to wake up, and we had to talk to the cunts for you."

"I would've talked them around," he says, puffing up his chest. Ted and I look at each other and start laughing. Wyn walks in from outside and Paddy comes in from a swim.

"Oh yeah, Vince? What would you have said?"

"I don't know, I would have thought of something, since I'm smarter than all of you put together." Ted and I laugh again. "You seen this, Wyn?" Vince asks him, waving the blue paper.

"Yes," says Wyn, his soft eyes look tired.

"So you're all in it together?" says Vince.

"Fuck off, Vince," I say. "It was all of ours."

"Not if I wasn't awake, it wasn't. Not if I never smoked any of it."

"You had some yesterday afternoon, you lying prick," says Ted. "You were the one ordering us to roll up, going on about how idyllic this place is, remember?"

"No."

"Oh, this is ridiculous," says Ted.

"Nothing we can do about it now," says Wyn. "I don't want to be stuck here all week with you arguing either. I told you, all of you, the band was to be drug free. But none of you would listen. None of you ever listen to me in any case. There's rules for you two," he points at Vince and I, "and there's rules for the rest of us. All I ever wanted to do," his eyes start watering and he picks his guitar up, "was to play music and have fun."

He looks outside, light shines in his face, stubble around his mouth. "We made an agreement remember? We were all going to be in London in twelve months. That was a year and a half ago. Instead we're stuck in this shit hole arguing with each other. I don't care who takes responsibility." He kicks a chair and walks out and down the stairs.

The Kombi putters into the carpark and starts high-revving once Darc pulls to a stop. Been hanging for this sound all week. I spent most of the time in the water away from the bad mood of the others. We carry all the gear down the steps while Vince argues with the manager about money. I jump in the van and sand falls out of my thongs and onto the floor. There's small blisters where the straps rub. We putt up the hill between the paperbarks. Darc stops at a lookout to watch the ocean, but I just want to get out of here. Vince and the other boys speed by up and over the hill. On the radio are fire warnings, like a roll call for all the towns in the area. I'm happy to be with Darc, just me and him.

"Get some new jeans, mate?"

"Yeah, thought I'd let my hair down," he says, waving his hand over his balding head. "I got out of it. I failed the test, Bon, you bloody beauty. No nasho for me!"

"What'd ya do?" I ask, feeling really happy for him.

"I did what you said. They play a recording, to test your hearing. They change the volume and ask if you can still hear it. I told them I'm a roadie and my hearing is damaged."

"That's true."

"Fuck you, mate." He hands me a joint. I take a long toke, the tingling sensation relaxing my muscles. A dead fox on the road.

"Then they give you a sight test. I passed that one, to make it seem proper. Then I fell over in the balancing test. There were heaps of people there, half of the cunts looked like they were ready to get blown up. You gunna share that thing?" He yells. Over the engine noise as we go uphill. "Anyone would think you haven't smoked all week."

"I haven't," I say. "We were raided."

"*What?*" He looks over, frowning, his little arms over the steering wheel.

"Cops came in after you left, found the stash, gave us a court order. Vince was asleep, he tried to weasel his way out it. Said the weed wasn't his."

"That silver tongued prick. He was the one who kept nagging us to buy it." Cows munch in the fields. A farmer waters small trees with a water tank rigged onto his motorbike. A green sign pointing to Sunshine. Up that road is where Mum and Dad and Dereck and I first lived when we arrived from Scotland. Mum drove Dad to the station. I sat on Dad's lap and we sang songs together. He taught me some drum beats, tapping on his thighs.

I see myself in the side mirror. My bloodshot eyes, messy hair and three day growth. My feet up on the dash. Off to court again. I'm such a piece of shit. Everywhere I turn, everything I do. I promised Mum and Dad I'd never get busted again. Ruined my relationship with Suzy. A hitch-hiker on the side of the road, swivels as we pass.

"Should we stop, Darc?"

"No room, mate," he says. "Hey, I've been thinking. You know that arts student, what's her name...Char..."

"Charmaine."

"Yeah, she said her parents, or her uncle, had a holiday home in Jan Juc."

"And her dad was a cop," I say. "You reckon she told her dad, and then he rang the Victorian cops?"

"Maybe she told him by accident?" he says, slowing to a set of lights. "You know what the pigs are like."

"I'll ask Vicki, she'll know. Don't tell Vince, though. Don't want to give him another excuse to try and get out of it."

Back to the shade of the figs of Dalgety Street. Heaps of cars parked outside our apartment block. On the verge a crowd of people holding microphones, a TV cameraman as well. The neighbours on the balcony. Darc drives out the back. At the top of the stairs is Gabby, and next to her is Suzy. She's wearing all white, with a white hand bag. She waves to me. *I remember we slept in. Suzy was late for work. She jumped into the bread van. There was no passenger seat. We were driving across Fremantle Bridge and I looked across and she was sitting on the loaves of bread, so cute, my little cream sandwich. Her soft skin, her little bit of makeup. I came home from work, and would see her shoes on the floor. The way they were thrown told me how her day went.* I step out of the van and three people run up and shove microphones in my face. I recognise them from Go-Set, and RAM. One of them is Ian Meldrum, always scratching for a story.

"How do you respond to the drug possession charges?" asks Ian. *Fuck, this is out of control,* I think to myself.

"The Valentines are the first band in Australia to be charged with drug possession, how does that feel?" the woman from RAM asks me. Her voice is excited, and she's pushed from the side. I try to walk to the bottom of the staircase. Through the breezeway I see Vince shooting his mouth off to other journalists, a big group of fans listening in.

"Bon, will you be pleading guilty or not guilty to the charges?" I look up at the sky. May as well say something.

"They should realise that what we do is right for us. We respect a lot of things about their job, but they shouldn't persecute whole groups of people just for being different." They all look amazed. Quite impressed myself. "The government deserves a few ripples. What year is it? 1950? They'll be the last to legalise homosexuality, and pot will be the same." I can feel my heart beat faster and my face get hot, my ears go red. I pick up a couple of guitar cases Darc has unloaded and climb the steps. At the top I put them down, and hug Suzy. A lightning feeling goes between us.

"Hello Tweety," I say, smiling.

"Hi Bon," she says. Gabby goes and talks to Darc.

"Did you get my letter?" I ask.

"No. What letter?" she says, looking confused. *Bloody* post office.

"Don't matter, good to see you," I say. "Let's go inside."

"Aren't you happy to see me?"

"Yes. Of course. What makes you think that?"

"You looked shocked."

"Well, you would be too if you had to deal with *them*."

"I arrived on Friday, and Gabby said you'd be back today." Her voice is big for her little body.

"Well. Here I am." I say. "Would you like a cup of tea?" The boys come and go dropping off gear, talking about the journalists. "You have something smudged on your knee." I bend over and touch her smooth, white calves. She licks her finger and wipes the smudge away. "Looks like paint from the balcony."

"Gabby says you were caught with marijuana? That true?" She tilts her head sideways. Her blue eyes meet mine.

"Yes."

"What's going to happen?"

"Go to court, probably get a record," I say.

"You don't care?"

"Yes. I care. But there's nothing I can do about it."

"What other drugs do you take?" she says, pressing the tea bag against the side of the cup.

"I've had heroin once."

"Anything else?"

"No."

"You've changed so much, Bon." She sits slowly on the chair, holding the cup in two hands. Vince enters. He smiles at Suzy, she doesn't smile back. He's sweating on his face, his armpits and chest.

"Hello Suzy," he says, his voice rising and falling.

"Hello Vincent," she says.

"How are we?"

"Very well, thank you, Vincent." She blinks. Her teeth are straight. She brushes lint off her skirt.

"You still upset about the..." I shake my head at him. "Oh, for fuck's sakes." He walks out. "Stuck up moll," he yells, his voice fading.

"Creep," she says. He tried to crack onto her in Freo once. He was giving us a lift and I was inside getting some things.

"Have you been going to church?" she asks, a hopeful look on her face.

"Oh yeah, of course," I say. "I go everyday, I pray to God he'll put an end to all this misery."

"Bon, sarcasm doesn't suit you." I bite my bottom lip. She's right. "Nobody is asking you to live the way you do. You can ask for forgiveness anytime. I know about the gang-bangs Bon." Her face contorts.

"Who told you that?"

"Was obvious, Bon. You think I'm stupid? There's no way we're getting married if you keep going on like this. Ever since that day at Terry's on Petra Street. Remember? You were meant to be rehearsing. You and Sharon Jarvis. Remember?" Her voice raises a little. I square up to her.

"What do you expect, Suzy? I can't be with someone for three years and all we do is...kiss."

"You said we were going to get married. You were going to wait for me."

"Things change Suzy."

"So you were lying?" she asks.

"No, I wasn't."

"What about the other girls then? You think I'm going to let you screw whoever you want? You know, I think your problem is you have this romantic idea about yourself. You think everyone's going to be in love with you, all the time. It doesn't work like that. I'm glad I never let you—"

"You know what? Stuff this," I say. "It's true, it's *all* true. I fucked up. You're right. You win, Suzy. I give up." The taste of bourbon in my mouth. I'm crying. She sits there playing with the button on her sleeve. A car horn beeps outside. The red headed neighbour who *must* park in *his* spot.

FRATERNITY
ADELAIDE — 1973

"Spot me a pie, Uncle?" I ask. He's squatting so he's eye level with the warmer. His leather jacket hangs outside his legs, touching his boots. A harmonica pokes out his chest pocket. He strokes his beard and looks like a wizard.

"A pie, eh? Good choice." His voice is muffled through his bushy beard. "What kind of pie you want?" He points inside the glass. "Steak, steak and kidney, steak and mushroom..."

"Steak is good—" I say.

"Chicken, chicken and vegetable, lamb..."

"*Steak. Just steak.*"

"Steak," he says, standing, throwing his head back, opening his eyes wide as if my split second decision was taken too hastily.

"I'll pay you back as soon as I can, and the rest of the money I owe ya." He fobs me off as the bakery lady comes and grabs the pies and slips them into paper bags.

Asks Uncle, "You're sure you want steak? I'm getting lamb. You want a coffee as well?"

"Take away?" the woman behind the counter asks. Flour covers all of her chest. Uncle and I look at Bruce and J.B. whose faces are lit up by the light of the dessert slice cabinet. Behind them, tables and chairs, all empty.

"You want sauce?" she asks Uncle.

"I'm saucy enough," he says. He pays and we walk outside. Autumn in Adelaide, summer yellow turning green. Double storey buildings with balconies. Cars parked all along at an angle. The hills way off. A freezing wind blows in from the ocean. The band's dog Clutch comes running up and starts begging.

"What happened with the trailer of bricks?"

"Oh yeah, well." Uncle sits on one of the chairs between the footpath and the road. "After I unloaded them all on her front lawn, stacked them neatly, blisters on my hands, she comes up to me — from you to your pie wrapper away — and tells me she doesn't want that colour any longer. That I need to load them back onto the trailer. I told her she'd already paid for them."

"You didn't even lay them?"

"Nah, they're in the trailer." He points across the road. Beneath a gum tree his white ute and trailer, triple parked. My yellow motorbike is next to John's truck. John's our drummer. Bruce and J.B. join us at the table. "Good pies, huh?" Uncle asks. A rattling of paper bags. He hasn't even taken a bite yet, he's rotating it around, deciding the best entry point. We've got our mouths full, steam floating out our mouths and the bitten pastry. We eat in silence when the bakery woman comes out, broom in hand. She apologises and says, "*Unfortunately* these tables and chairs are for dine-in customers only." Clutch wags his tail at her. Bruce rolls his eyes and tells her, "Okay," and we all go to get up as she walks back inside.

Bruce is our bass player and band organiser. He can grow a beard. All I can muster is goatee and some advanced bum-fluff. Nope, if he fully shaves he's back to beard in four days and trimming his nose hairs every morning. Sometimes he misses a few and they glisten in the light when he's talking. The rest of his hair had long since disappeared on top of his scalp, but he makes up for it everywhere else. His brown eyes are warm, but they'll go all fiery if you cross him. That don't usually last long, as he moves on quick. His oval shaped glasses sit neatly on his nose and he pushes them up whenever he bursts into a laughing fit. He's like my big brother. When you talk to him, everything seems like a big hassle, but secretly he's working out a way to make everything cool.

He and John are from Adelaide, and they dragged us over here from Sydney. There's three Johns. John the drummer, and John, or J.B. the keyboard player. Uncle's a John too, but we never think of him by that name.

"What's going on with these arts government gigs, Bruce?" I ask.

"Oh, don't get me started," he says, wiping pastry shards off his belly. Bits dangle in his beard. "Bunch of imbeciles. It'll be worth it once we get on the road, but at the moment I'm busier than a one armed taxi driver with crabs." His puffy cheeks lift before he's finished his sentence. We all laugh. The woman inside gives us evil eyes.

"You watch Humphries last night too?" asks Uncle.

"Yep, what a funny bastard. Anyway, I've been having these daily phone conversations with the arts guy. They're going to pay us properly, but there's all these stupid rules they've concocted." He scrunches up his pie wrapper and pulls his custard tart close. He sits on the front edge of his chair and leans on his elbows on the table. "For starters," he says, pulling on his little finger as if to make a point, "no girlfriends."

"*What?*"

"Yeah, I'm not shitting you. No girlfriends, wives or flings, they reckon."

"Why not?"

"They say they're not paying for extra people, and they don't want us rooting around causing trouble in the towns."

"That's bullshit," says John, the drummer.

"We have to play at strict times and finish on the dot," says Bruce. A postman rides up, dismounts and pats Clutch.

"That's easy," I say, taking my last bite.

"We have to have afternoon tea with the oldies a few times."

"Okay."

"No swearing at any time."

"Fuck off."

"No drugs." Everyone looks at Uncle. He smokes a lot, but doesn't drink. Out comes the bakery woman again, her face looks like a smashed up truck.

"I'm not going to ask you lot one more time. If you don't leave I'm going to call the police."

"That's proprietorial discrimination," says Bruce.

"I don't care what it is," she says.

"Call the cops then," says Bruce. He turns back to us "...And one more thing, this bureaucrat named Richard has to come with us. On the bus, staying in the same hotels, eating at the same restaurants." The bakery woman folds her arms and goes inside.

"What is this, *The Godfather*?" I ask.

"Have you finished it yet?" asks Bruce. The roar of a blue Monaro drives up the road and back again, parks next to John's truck.

"Nearly." I put on my best Italian accent. "My reading is like-a-tortoise. It is slow, and takes very long time. Very long time."

"I wanna read it after you, Bon," says Uncle.

"When do we leave, Bruce?" asks J.B.

"Tomorrow. Can you tell Mick?" Mick's our guitarist. "I already told Ralph, he's getting the bus ready." Ralph is our roadie. We call him Ralph because he looks like a cartoon character. The bus came on the boat, back from England last week. England was our failed attempt at ruling the world as rock and roll stars.

"Bon bloody Scott," I hear. Walking towards us is Pat Pickett, from Melbourne. He's tall, gaunt, and sick looking.

"Well, if it isn't *the one and only*. What brings you here, mate?" I stand up and shake his hand and introduce him to everyone.

"Had enough of Melbourne," he says. "So I got my last dole cheque, and I thought I'd come see you. Jeez, it's quiet here. They all said Adelaide was quiet, but I didn't think it would be *this* quiet. You can hear a nun fart." Everyone laughs except Bruce. Pat's missing some front teeth and the ones he's got are yellow and black. "Haven't seen you since the Valentines' last shows, when was that? Three years ago or something?" He grabs a chair from the other table.

"Yep. We've been to London and back since then."

"Fair dinkum? I heard yous won Hoadley's but hardly nothin' since. What else happened?"

"We flew over. Most of us. Put the bus and all our gear on a boat. Stayed there for two years, did a tour of Germany, but we came back with our tail between our legs."

"Jeez, you look different mate, bet you're still getting your end wet every second day. Got any spare?" says Pat.

"Nah, I'm married now. Well, only just," I say.

"That good, hey?" he says, pretending to box with me. "Let's go to the pub and play pool."

"Not right now," I say, "but come over later. I'm staying on Norwood parade. The big red brick joint, you can't miss it."

"Have a look at this, have a look at this," he says. He cocks his leg, puts a lighter in front of his crack and lets a fart go up in blue flame. We all laugh again, except Bruce, who looks inside the bakery. We all stand up and start leaving. I offer Bruce a lift on the back of the motorcycle but he says no. Says I ride like a maniac. My little yellow Suzuki, too small to hurt anyone. At the traffic lights I drag the cars and lean over the handlebars and feel good and free and alone. The wide streets are handy because you can see cars coming from side roads and swerve to miss the ones that don't see you. By ten at night you have the roads to yourself. Bruce says he won't be coming to my funeral if I crash. Says I could hardly walk when I got home the other night. I never feel *that* drunk at the time, just the next day when I wake up.

Our house is wedged between two hotels and a chicken shop. There's a front door with some sash windows, but we only ever use the back door, down the gravel driveway. I park on the grass next to the outdoor dunny. There's a big tree that fills the back yard where toadstools grow in winter. Anne and Cheryl, Bruce and J.B.'s wives, have some herbs growing near the clothesline. We never lock the back door.

My turn to clean the kitchen and bathroom. I put a *Them* record on and get into it. A family of magpies come to the door and start singing. I give them some mince and have a little sing along. *In my mind I see Jonathon's club in Kings Cross. I was auditioning for Fraternity. I entered the front door and heard the owner saying he doesn't want some Valentine joining. My heart sank. Bruce said, "Bon joins or I leave."* I walk down the hallway, dark figures move in the frosted glass of the front door. In my bedroom I pick up clothes off the floor, smelling them to see if they're clean. There's a murmur in the bed, giving me a shock. Irene's golden hair all over the pillow. I sit on the bed. On the bedside table packets of tablets, an empty glass, a half done drawing and our wedding photo. A white envelope on the floor. I pick it up.

"That's not yours," she says, her voice like a broken motor.

"I'm putting it on the table for you. What are you doing home?"

"Can't you tell I'm sick?" she says.

"Nothing unusual there," I say.

"Very funny, nothing unusual about you being home. Found a job yet?"

"Yep, we're going on the road tomorrow, this government gig. I'll be able to pay you back..." She starts heaving and coughing then finds the phlegm in her lungs and spews it up, grabs a tissue and wipes the green into the white. She rearranges the blanket, warm air and her smell fills the room. I lie next to her on my back. I find my copy of Barry McKenzie and start reading. Maybe this'll cheer her up.

I have a little creature
I guess you can call him a pet
If there's something wrong with him
I don't have to call a vet
He goes wherever I do
Whether sleeping or awake
God ever help me if I lose my one eyed trouser snake
Oh me one eyed trouser snake, oh me one eyed trouser snake...

I sing and sing my heart out and make the bed bounce. No reaction from Irene. We drifted apart in London. I flick the book forward a few pages. Maybe this'll work.

I was down by the old Bondi Pier
Cracking tubes of ice cold beer
With a bucket full of prawns upon my knee
When I swallowed the last prawn
I had a technicolor yawn
And chundered in the old pacific sea.

Her shoulders jolt a little in the blanket. I place my hand on her thigh. "Hug me," she says. My heart jolts. She must be really sick as we haven't hugged in weeks. I curve my crotch to her bum with the blanket between us, pull my chest to her back. She is delicate. Her hair smells like lollies and it tickles my face. Her body jumps as she coughs again. Car noises outside. "I went and visited Vicki this morning, on my way home from work." Vicki is Uncle's girlfriend, the girl from Melbourne who lived in our apartment block. She moved back to Adelaide and introduced me to Irene at the Largs Pier one night.

"How is she?" I ask.

"Not good, she's in the hospital. They're going to keep her in there for at least a week, maybe longer."

"What happened?"

"She went to the doctor last week." Her voice is warming up. "She told him she was having evil thoughts, mainly at night. The doctor, can you believe it, said that she might actually be evil, and gave her all this medication. She said the meds didn't do anything and gave her more nightmares. But she went back a few days later with the plan of knocking herself off. So the doctor gave her another hundred and forty pills. *Drongo*." She coughs and grabs my hand. I feel a woody starting. She speaks deadpan, and to the wall.

"So she goes home, eats a whole packet of raspberry shortcakes, and pops the bottle of pills. All of them. Anita says she walked in and Vicki looked like a stunned mullet, lying on the lounge room floor. So Vicki says, *I'll go see the doctor,* cause she didn't wanna disturb the baby. She gets to the doctors. Oh, and she caught the tram, this is the bloody detail she includes. The same doctor, the one who gave her the pills, and she starts vomiting all these capsules and biscuits. The doctor rings the ambulance and says she had a brush with death, like the grim reaper with a broom instead of a sickle."

"Far out Irene. *Far out*," I say. "What are we going to do?"

"What do you mean?"

"She can't do it all on her own. Is Anita going to look after her?"

"Uncle isn't going to do it. He doesn't know which way is up half the time." I thrust my doodle into her bum a few times.

"Stop it," she says, "I'm sick. Don't start thinking we're back on again. I told you I'm looking for somewhere else to live. You blew it when you stole the rent money off the fridge." I roll off and onto my back. *At Singapore airport. Irene and me argued for hours. It was a bad time for everyone.*

"I might be gone by the time you get back from the country. Might have found a place in Prospect."

"Prospect? What'd you wanna live in Prospect for?"

"Why do you care? You've got this Margaret woman, or Silver, or whatever she's calling herself these days. You can live with her."

"I only slept with her once. It meant nothing." I see Margaret's beautiful face, like an Italian goddess.

"Oh, really? She's married too you know," she says.

"You haven't filed for divorce yet."

DEAR SUZY,

LONG TIME. HOW'S LIFE? I HEARD YOU MOVED BACK TO PERTH AND OPENED A FEW SHOPS THERE. GOT SICK OF MELBOURNE HEY? MUST BE TWO YEARS SINCE WE LAST SPOKE. ~~YOU SINGLE?~~

WHERE DO I START? WELL, AFTER THE VALENTINES SPLIT I WAS KICKING AROUND SYDNEY AND RAN INTO A BLOKE NAMED BRUCE. HE AND HIS BAND THE LEVI SMITH CLEFS HAD A SHOW HAPPENING AT A CLUB CALLED JOHNATHON'S. THE REST OF THE BAND DIDN'T WANT ME AT FIRST BECAUSE I WAS A VALENTINE, BUT BRUCE CONVINCED THEM AND WE PLAYED AT JOHNATHON'S EVERY NIGHT FOR ABOUT SIX MONTHS. AFTER THAT WE MOVED TO ADELAIDE BECAUSE OUR MANAGER HAMISH SAID WE COULD SET UP IN THE HILLS AND GET SOME SONGS TOGETHER AND RECORD. WASN'T LONG AND WE WON HOADLEY'S AND NEXT THING WE WERE OFF TO ENGLAND, SO IRENE AND I GOT MARRIED CAUSE WIVES COULD COME FOR FREE. WE PUT THE BUS ON THE SHIP WITH RALPH AND J.B. AND HIS DOG AND THE REST OF US FLEW.

THERE WERE NINETEEN OF US LIVING IN THIS TOWNHOUSE. ALL THE BAND MEMBERS, THEIR WIVES OR GIRLFRIENDS, A FEW ROADIES AND THE DOG. ABOUT A YEAR IN, THERE WERE A FEW EXTRAS WITH SOME BABIES POPPING OUT. THERE WERE SOME CRAZY TIMES, BUT WE COULDN'T GET HALF THE SHOWS WE WANTED CAUSE ALL THE LONDON MANAGERS WERE ONLY LOOKING OUT FOR THEMSELVES AND THEY RECKONED WE WERE FIVE YEARS TOO LATE FOR THE MUSIC WE WERE PLAYING. COMES A TIME WHEN ALL THE BLOKES HAVE TO GET A JOB CAUSE WE'RE NOT PLAYING ANYWHERE, BUT IT WAS GREAT TO BE LIVING IN LONDON. I'LL TAKE YOU THERE ONE DAY.

SO NOW WE'RE BACK IN ADELAIDE. GOT THIS GOVERNMENT TOUR IN THE COUNTRY FOR BIT OF DOUGH. MUM SAYS I HAVE TO BE BACK IN FREO FOR CHRISTMAS SO MAYBE WE CAN SPEND A DAY TOGETHER? GO TO THE MOVIES OR SOMETHING?

CATCH YOU SOON TWEETY,
LOVE,
BON.

The chrome Fraternity tour bus brakes and squeaks and hisses. The door opens slowly at first, then fast. Ralph, wiping hair out of his eyes, waits for it to open while Bruce, J.B. and I wait with all our gear on the footpath. He jumps from the bottom step, over the gutter and onto the curb. He says a quick hello and starts loading up. The government guy, Richard, rocks up, wearing a tweed jacket with black elbow patches, red corduroy trousers and a paisley cravat. He shakes our hands. I ask if he likes the name Dick, and he says no. He jumps on the bus, sitting up the front. After a bit of arguing about whether or not Clutch can come, we get going.

First stop is Aldgate where we pick up Mick and John and Uncle. The bus struggles up the hill through tall trees and small villages. A motorbike speeds past us--*Margaret and*

I rode in fog. It was freezing cold, with low visibility--Ralph steers us on the long zig-zag to Strathalbyn, the engine brakes hissing, bolts of lightning and lines and lines of vineyards. From Strathalbyn we cross the Murray River, driving the bus onto a chain-ferry. We follow the Coorong and pull up at the Millicent Town Hall, where we are to play tonight. From here we criss-cross farming country to Bordertown, Renmark, then head west to Clare. The days are mild, the nights are cold. We keep to ourselves. We play well and stick to Richard's rules, ducking off to have a joint or two every so often. Everything is going swimmingly until Richard decides to make a little speech. Before we get off the bus in Port Pirie, he blocks off the door, all suited up, and asks us to listen for a few minutes. Outside kids ride circles and the air is hazy with dust.

"Gentlemen," he says, clearing his throat and rocking his tie side to side, "a few words, if I may." His voice is bit like Mickey Mouse's. "I have to admit, when I was given this assignment, I had my reservations." He hops on his toes at the end of every sentence. "I had watched your outfit on television, and judging you merely by the way you dressed I thought you were a bunch of degenerate no hopers. I went out of my way to be on this assignment as I was certain you gents would break the rules and cause headaches wherever you went. My reservations were unfounded. Throughout this tour I have found Fraternity to be one of the most professional groups I have ever worked with, certainly within the arts community. When I return to Adelaide I intend on writing the highest recommendation I can." I look around. Behind a chair, Uncle is rolling a joint. John is looking out the window, a pissed off expression on his face. He's still annoyed no girlfriends are allowed. J.B. is asleep. Mick and Bruce are listening, and they look at one another with raised eyebrows. I take a sip of whisky from a small bottle I have stashed.

"That mean we can have a few drinks tonight?" sings out Bruce. "I'm tonguing."

"Not so fast Brucey-boy—" says Richard. Ralph opens the front door and we shove past him before he finishes.

You can never get lost in Pirie, because of the smelter stack. In the air, a mixture of smoke, and dust and salt. My nostrils are instantly itchy. A swarm of oldies outside the Central Hotel, a brick corner setup. They enter one by one, like bees in a hive. Inside, the dining hall has arched windows and exposed beams. On the walls are copies of famous shearing and forestry paintings. Bruce, Uncle and I sit together next to Carol and Len, a couple from Port Augusta. They smell of sherry and cigarettes and order two bottles of shiraz. Len is thin, his skin sags and tiny red veins look ready to burst in his cheeks and nose. Carol crosses her big arms over her belly, below a scarf and about five necklaces. Her face is heavy with make up. She wears a brown wig and stuffs tissues in her bra. I get the feeling Carol and Len could drop off at any moment. Carol leans in and whispers something in Len's ear. She points, leans back and laughs loudly. A silver haired man in blue overalls.

The room fills up and it's loud with voices and chairs scraping and clangs from the kitchen. Before we finish our drinks Len tops us up. Bruce puts his hand over the glass and says they're different kinds of wine, but Len frowns at him and starts pouring. Carol takes a mouthful and says, "Cheers." Uncle holds a wine glass up to the light, like he's figuring out how it's made.

"Bet you boys can't wait to get out of here," Carol says, the glass still in front of her face, "full of stuck up farmers who think they own everything." She finishes the wine in another gulp, leaving lipstick all over the glass.

"We—" Bruce starts.

"We'll sort em out, won't we, Len?" she says. "You have to make your own fun."

"We've been here before," I say, my mouth moving funny from the wine. "About two years ago, wasn't it, Bruce?" He's reading the menu, his glasses on the ridge of his nose. “Bruce, remember when we caught the train to Perth?”

“O’course,” he says, his face lighting up. Len offers him a cigarette, which he accepts. “I’m not telling the story now, though, it’s too long.”

“Oh, go on, we’ve got all day,” says Carol, wiping ash off the table. Bruce looks out the stained glass window, gathering his thoughts.

“The band was doing some shows in Perth,” he says, “but there was no back-line equipment there, you know, P.A., fold backs, mixing desks and all that stuff.” Smoke swirls above our heads.

“Probably still isn’t,” I say, holding back a sneeze.

“I’ve always wanted to go to Perth,” says Carol. “Never got around to it.”

“So Bon and I got asked to put the van on the train. He didn’t need any encouragement to go on a road trip home for a few weeks.”

“You’re from Perth, Bon?” asks Len.

“Yeah, Freo,” I say, “but I was born in Scotland.”

“Why didn’t you drive?”

“The road isn’t sealed all the way,” says Bruce, ashing his fag. “Everyone else got to fly. We packed up the van and drove up here from Adelaide. There was a few hours between loading the van and then the train leaving.”

“No,” I tell him. “The van went on one train and we went on the passenger train, *remember*? We had to wait overnight in Kalgoorlie for the van to catch up to us.”

“Yeah, yeah, that’s right,” says Bruce, a frown fading from his face. A waiter drops a tray of glasses. I see Mick and J.B. at another table. They start bringing out soup and bread. “We had a few hours to kill, so we went to a pub down the road there. Outside the pub were rows and rows of motorbikes, Harleys mainly.”

“You didn’t want to go in.”

"Well, I was wearing pretty much what I'm wearing now."

"I don't blame him," says Len. "I got beat up once in Port Augusta."

"*Bloody Ron,* he drags me inside, and the whole place goes quiet. We go up to the bar and order some beers. There's about thirty of them, black leather, tattoos, beards," says Bruce. "Some of them were playing pool, but most of them were watching us. And what does Ron do? He goes up to the pool table, puts money down and challenges them. Ten minutes later, they're buying him rounds of beer, getting along like old mates."

"We nearly missed the train," I say, buttering my bread. "We had a travel allowance from Hamish. Remember Bruce?"

"That's right, fifty bucks each, wasn't it?"

"How long does the train take?" asks Carol.

"Two nights to Kalgoorlie," says Bruce.

"It's all a bit of a blur, we were on acid most of the way," I say.

"Oh yeah," says Bruce, a cheeky smile coming over him. "We sat in our cabin all night tripping off our heads, watching the stars out the window, with all these emus chasing the train. At about four in the morning, we stopped near Maralinga for fifteen minutes or so. Near where they had the nuclear tests." Len grunts. Uncle, a pacifist, opens his eyes up wide, a kind of nuclear bomb exploding in his head. The waiters start bringing out the meat and three veg. I gotta wee real bad. Carol keeps topping our drinks up.

Bruce continues, "Every now and then, you'd see wild cats watching the train, *freaky things.* We got going again and the sun started to rise, and Ron and I stood in the passageway spinning out, didn't we, Ron?"

"This strange fog," I say.

"The sun was huge, the biggest I've ever seen it. All these greys, and oranges, and purples. The bushes in the distance stationary, the ones up close all blurry."

"The train guard was watching with us."

"That's right, he said he'd never seen anything like it, and he'd worked on the train for ten years. Anyway, we moved into the dining car for breakfast, all these brass fittings and white table cloths. We're sitting there tripping out and this ex-Vietnam guy...we'd seen him the night before...he was off the planet... he was shoving his fist in everyone's faces...trying to pick a fight. The train workers tried to restrain him, but that made it worse. He was smoking these tiny cigars. Ron and I thought we were gunna cop it, cause we look like hippies..."

"*You* thought we were gunna cop it," I say, mopping up the soup with a bread roll. He had a huge nose, I remember that much. Carol and Len are listening. Another woman next to Bruce is listening in as well.

"...There was a whole bunch of them in uniform...this nasho's waving his fist at people and we're coming off the LSD. All the other passengers are freaking out and moving back to their cabins and what do you reckon Ron does?"

"He punched him?" says Len.

"Len!" says Carol.

"No," says Bruce, "he stands up, sticks out his hand and says, *G'day mate, my name's Bon Scott, what's your name?"* Bruce sits back, smiles, closes his eyes, and shakes his head from side to side.

"He just wanted someone to talk to," says Carol.

"Yeah, he was a bit messed up, but he was a nice bloke really," I say, watching the sediment in the bottom of my glass as I finish it. I'm feeling a bit dizzy.

"There were fights all over the country at the time, all these army guys and protesters fighting," says Bruce, starting to slur.

"There still are," says Len.

"Yeah," says Bruce, sweat on his brow, "so we sat there talking to this guy for about three hours, buying shots of whisky, he and Ron getting along like a house on fire. Then all the other passengers come back for lunch and this guy stands up and says, *Listen here, you lot, have a good look at these two, they've got more guts than the whole lot of you put together, they can think and act for themselves which is more than I can say for the rest of yas*, or something like that." Bruce tucks into his food. Len and Carol are half way through a smoke. The waiters start collecting our plates. A loud car drives by. *Me and Mum and Dereck and Graeme were on the same train. I was just a kid. The land was as big as the ocean.*

"Is that it?" asks Carol, working a toothpick.

"What?" asks Bruce.

"Is that the end of the story?"

"Oh no. Get this," says Bruce. "This is my favourite bit. We get to Kalgoorlie, and we've got a night to kill before the train arrives with our van. We've got forty dollars or so to spend on a nice hotel with a bath. I wanted to have a full meal and a good night's sleep and Ron decides he wants to spend our allowance playing pool and getting pissed." They look at me.

"Man after my own heart," says Len.

"We only had about an hour sleep since we left Adelaide," says Bruce.

Interrupting him, I say, "Forget about that, I said, *Let's go for a walk, have some lunch, check out the red light district and worry about where we're gunna sleep later.*"

"I wasn't going to waste my money on whores though," says Bruce, pushing the last of his lamb in his mouth.

"I'd been there a few times," I say. "There are these rows and rows of tin shacks where the girls get the miners to come in." Bruce is all excited by the story now. Carol tops us up again.

"Yeah, so we go from pub to pub. The Oriental, the Commercial and the York. I think we got kicked out of a couple. Gets to about eight at night and I says to Ron, *Where are we going to sleep?* He goes away and comes back ten minutes later and says he's found somewhere for a dollar. In disbelief I follow him out the back of the Commercial and there's all these sheds with these steel framed beds. No mattresses, just springs. No floor, just dirt. It's boiling hot inside and there's no light either, just some tiny holes letting in the star light."

"We didn't need a blanket," I tell Carol and Len.

Bruce says, "I don't know why I went along with it, I think we were starting to run out of money by then, so I say to him, *Right, well, I'm not sleeping until much later,* and we left our stuff there and went back to the pub and kept drinking until after close."

"I had to drag you out of there. And then you kept trying to walk off into the desert," I tell him.

"I don't remember that bit," he says. "I remember it took us ages to open the door. In the end we get inside and it's pitch black because our eyes can't adjust and I'm feeling my way around." He waves his hands around in front of him, and continues, "And I feel a face, and then some shoulders. And I didn't wanna feel any further, and I say to Ron," his voice goes all high pitched, "*Ron, someone's sleeping in my bed.* So I tried another bed and disturbed someone, I must have tried about five different beds, stumbling around everywhere. And I say to Ron again, *someone's sleeping in my bed,* and you'll never guess what Ron says, I don't know where he comes up with this stuff." Bruce looks us all in the eye, lifts his elbows out wide, making fists in front of his chest that he bounces with each word, and says, "All I hear from the pitch black is Ron's voice whispering, *Someone's been eating my porridge as well...*" Bruce flings his head back, veins popping out around his temples, Carol's throat blocks and smoke comes out her nose. Len taps the table three times. They all look at me, expectant.

"We had to find another shed with no one in it," I say.

"Oh, it was classic," says Bruce, wiping tears from the outside of his eyes, "I'll never forget it."

I stand up, holding onto the back of the chair and the table. The room spins. Len grabs my arm and nods. I grin at him and make my way through the hall to the men's. I burp but keep my mouth shut and the stink comes out my nose. At the piss trough I brace myself with a hand overhead. In the mirror

I take some deep breaths and tell myself to keep it together. I wash my face and scrub my teeth with my finger to try to remove the red stains. In walks Richard, as chirpy as a willy wagtail. He doesn't seem to notice how drunk I am. Probably had a few himself. I get stuck with him for a few moments while he talks about how much he loves Australian towns.

The venue is a brand new white box building with wood paneling. You enter on the ground floor, go up a flight of stairs and then find your seat in the bowl shaped auditorium. The lights in the ceiling match the lights in the aisles. The chairs smell new. On the stage, Ralph the roadie works flat out. I say hello and jump up on the stage. We're due on in about half an hour. We play thirty minutes to the oldies, then have a break and then play to the kids.

Backstage, John is getting ready. He's pissed off about the rules and he's stuck on getting back to Adelaide tomorrow. In walks Bruce. He's got a girl on each of his arms, grinning like a goose. Two birds I've seen him with in Adelaide. John's face gets all angry, his arms are crossed.

"So this is why you didn't want any girlfriends or wives to come?" he says, a few sets of drum sticks in his hands. Bruce looks shocked.

"Hang on a sec, hang on," says Bruce. "I only just ran into them outside, they saw we were playing." The girls look like they want to leave.

"Bullshit, you didn't want any of the women here cause you didn't want Anne finding out," yells John, his Adam's apple rising and falling, a lump forming above his nose.

"I'm telling the fucking truth," says Bruce, the pitch of his voice getting higher. Uncle pokes his head in and says we're on in five.

"Well, fuck this," says John. "I'm ringing Sue, see if she wants to drive up for the night. I'm sick of all this rules bullshit. You wanna see if Carol wants to come, Mick?" he asks. Mick is standing up strapping his guitar on.

"Alright," he says.

"I'll see if J.B. wants to ask Cheryl, and Uncle wants to ask Vicki. You wanna ask Irene, Bon?" I miss Irene, but I'm not sure.

"What, you gunna ring them now?" I ask.

"We're about to go on," says Bruce.

"Oh, shut up, Bruce," says John. Bruce shakes his head, lets go of the girls and asks them to meet him afterward.

"You make up your own mind, John," says Bruce, "but if you screw this up and we don't get paid because of your bullshit, then don't blame me." Bruce picks up his bass and tunes it quickly, turning his back to John.

"That's right," says John, "it's never your fault, Bruce the blameless. Wanker. It's obvious you've been drinking," pointing to the red wine stain on his shirt.

"Alright, alright," says Uncle, thumbing his dungarees, his voice muffled by his beard. "That's enough, all hands on deck."

"You lads ready to go on?" asks Richard, coming in all excited. "Now remember," he says, "no swearing." He goes on stage and gives an introduction. J.B. is already out there, sitting at his organ. We open with *Seasons of Change,* our single. I play recorder in parts but the band doesn't really get it together. You can't see the audience. We all make mistakes at different times.

During *Grand Canyon Suites,* Uncle starts a harmonica solo, spinning and twirling around. The song builds up in the middle and he's getting lost in the music. J.B. is about to let rip when Uncle's foot misses the front of the stage and he goes flying into the first row. All these grannies shielding themselves from him. He jumps back up on stage quickly and finishes the song.

"Alright there, Uncle?" I ask him on the microphone. He gives me a thumbs up. "You all having a good time?" I ask the audience. No answer. "Alright, let's get this shit over with," and we play through *Raglan's Folly*. We finish with *Livestock* and jam out for a while at the end. The audience claps slowly, the lights brighten, we don't bow or wave. I want a drink straight away. Backstage we relax for a minute. Bruce says we should go to the pier. In walks Richard, he looks stressed out.

"What were you thinking?" he asks.

"Wh..what are you talking about?"

"The swearing. There's been complaints. You said *shit,* remember?" He's a foot away from me, looking really concerned.

"You've got to be joking, Dick."

"No, I'm not joking, Ron."

"Well, for fucks sakes," I say. "This is just bullshit, most of the oldies swear more than I do."

"*Rules are rules,* Mister." He runs his hand through his hair. "Don't let this happen again."

"C'mon, Ron," says Bruce, "let's go for a walk."

The sun beats bright on the quiet streets. The footpaths have large holes and cracks in them. The eaves of the shops are covered in cobwebs. Up ahead is a bottle shop. Bruce goes inside and I go to the phone booth.

"Hello Spunk, how are ya?"

"Oh, Ron, what do you want? I'm busy." Irene's voice sounds better.

"Sorry Irene, thought I'd give you a call. Haven't talked to you in nearly a week." Kids ride their bikes along the road. "John and Mick are ringing Sue and Carol, they're gunna drive up here to Port Pirie. You wanna join them?"

"No, Ron. I'm not coming. I don't have any money left after you stole the rent money."

"What?"

"The white envelope, dummy. You took it, didn't you?"

"No."

"Well, I can't find it anywhere. Disappeared the morning you left." A kind of painful feeling rushes through my chest, from one arm to the other.

"Maybe someone else took it?" I say.

"You're not getting out of this one, Bon. That's it." She hangs up. Fucking hell. I grip the handle as hard as possible, shaking it. Fuck.

Bruce stands outside the phone booth holding two paper bags. I tell him what happened. He says not to worry about it and we walk to the pier. White wooden barriers all along the left side. Grey boards tilt when you step on them. A cold wind blows. The water is dark with seaweed, but clears the further we walk out. Fishermen sit on the edge, little white eskies between them, buckets behind. Set lines are tied to the galvanised ladders. White sunlight rings sit below the surface. A pelican stands on the only light post. Two fishing boats and a trawler bounce against some old tyres.

At the end of the jetty there's a metal frame for weighing fish. A group of people stand looking over the edge. In the water you can see thousands of stingers and jellyfish. Their long tentacles sway in the current. Their tails are like flames if they touch your skin. Two young boys pace back and forth, wearing only undies. One of them says to the other, "Go in if you want, but I'm not going in, not with *those* stingers."

I take a swig from my quart of whisky and hand it to Bruce. I take my shirt off and tie my hair back. I take my boots off and roll my jeans up. My armpits stink.

"You going in, you crazy bastard?" asks Bruce. I raise my eyebrows at him and smile. The kid in his undies watches me, looks at my tattoos. A small ladder covered in seagull shit goes half way up the tower. My feet scrape on the rusted metal as I lean back and climb to the top. All along the pier, people are watching, shielding their eyes from the sun. I'm level with the roof of the tall cray boat. I hold onto a thin rod. A gust of wind blows and I wonder how deep the water is. The stingers are invisible from up here but I can make out a few jelly fish.

Bruce is chatting with the kids, his arms crossed. More and more people walk towards me. Too late to turn back now. I look up at the horizon. I think of Terry and the cliffs in Freo. I put my feet together and let go of the rod. My heart is pounding. I jump outward. My eyes widen. I throw my arms out wide, trying to keep my legs tight. Whirring in my ears, like an engine revving, louder and louder. Head first I fall and fall. I bring my hands together in front of my face. I slightly over pitch, the water smashing my ear drums. I dive deep and open my eyes. A school of herring. Ripples in the sand. I start breaststroking toward the pylons, toward the boat hulls. Pausing for a moment, I let out some bubbles, black figures lean on the edge of the pier.

On the surface I gasp for air and grab onto the ladder and go up a few steps. Mussels cling at the water level. Salt taste. My chest heaves. The little kid comes down the ladder and I work my way past him. At the top slithers of water weave through my chest hair. Applause erupts in the gathered crowd. I raise my hand and thank them, tell them all to come watch us, Fraternity, at the new venue a bit later. Bruce hands me my shirt and boots. We start heading to the shore, to the smoke stack pumping white, and I take a big gulp of whisky. The little kid from the steps keeps following us.

"I think he likes you, Ron," says Bruce. We reach the concrete ramp covered in sand. My feet are covered in sand. The boy grabs my hand. I squat down and put my hands on his shoulders and tell him we have to go. I look back a few times as we get closer to the auditorium. The kid stands there watching us.

"You're on in ten minutes," says Ralph. I run out to the bus and find my bag and put on a fresh pair of jeans, a large brown belt and a flannel shirt. I can feel the salt on my skin rubbing on the clean cotton. A big swig of whisky makes my body shake.

I run back inside and Richard is giving his introductory speech. We walk on to disjointed applause. This new building has a mechanical floor at the front of the stage that lowers and turns into a dance floor. About three hundred faces look at us wide eyed. There are two cops in each aisle. They stop the kids enjoying themselves.

We open with *Cool Spot*, a percussive song with loud guitar and organ solos. It's a song you can dance to, but the kids don't dare stand up. Our drummer plays much louder than in the sound check and everyone else creeps their volume up. We rip straight into *Livestock,* Bruce's walking bass-lines filling the room. He's wearing a black leather jacket and he's going for it, sweat shining on his forehead. His glasses keep slipping. Uncle presses a few pedals and spins off into his own world. His harmonica disappears into his beard. He sounds more like a guitar than a harp. The kids look bewildered. They've never heard a band this loud. Some look paralysed.

One of the boys in blue is chatting to Richard at the back of the room. Richard shakes his head and says something behind his cupped hand. At the end of the song Richard works his way to the side of the stage, grabs Bruce's attention and tells him to turn it down. I turn to the crowd and say, "Looks like we have a few what-nots here who want to tell us what to do." A few of the kids cheer. The cops shake their heads. Richard looks furious.

John counts us in for *Summerville* and I let myself go in the climax singing, *THIS IS MY HOME*, rising an octave for the ending. After the song I ask one of the girls in the front row how she's doing. She gets all embarrassed. I look as many kids in the eyes as I can and say, "We are under orders not to say shit, or fuck, or any other swear words so if you hear any let me know and I'll tell your parents." They all laugh. A few gasp. One of the cops points at me and makes a throat cutting motion.

We finish the set and waiting backstage are Carol and Sue and

Vicki. No Irene or Bruce's wife Anne. The couples pair off and go out the back door. Richard comes up and tells Bruce he's washing his hands of us, that he'll try to get the money, but no guarantees. I go to the toilet and when I return Bruce has buggered off. Four cops come in. They wear black uniforms and their trousers are neatly creased. They crowd around and smell like starch. The big guy grabs my arm and pushes me into the manager's office.

They throw me in a chair and lock the door. The grey haired one sits on the table with his legs dangling. He adjusts his belt. His gut hangs out of his shirt. He takes his hat off and hangs it on the picture on the table. The big one is behind me, with his hands on my shoulders, and the other two on each side. All their balls are at my eye level, I could easily punch their lollie bags back into the deli.

"What's your name, son?" Grey Hair asks.

"Bon, Bon Scott," I say, looking at his shoes.

"This is Constable Mackenzie, Jones, and Roberts."

"Cuntstables," I say, nodding.

"I'm Sergeant Holt. You want to tell us why you elected to swear at the audience?"

"I wasn't swearing at..."

"Your breath smells like whisky, you little hippy. Thought hippies don't drink?" says Jones, trying to sound threatening.

"I'm not a hippy," I tell them.

"The government official, Richard," says Holt, swinging one leg, "he informs me you knew full well you were not to swear on stage. Do you recall these provisions? Do you think we would have let you anywhere near Pirie otherwise?" The big guy tightens his grip on my shoulders. I swivel, look up and see his boogie filled nostrils.

"You going to arrest me?" I ask. I'm starting to get worried. What exactly do they want?

"Shut your hole," says Jones. I inch forward in my seat using my arms. The grip tightens on my shoulders and he pulls me back. Grey Hair mumbles behind his hand to Roberts who then goes out of the room.

"What's this stupid parrot tattoo on your arm for?" says Jones. He has a scar between his upper lip and nose. Roberts comes back in and says, "There's no one out there." He gives his revolver to Holt.

"Where the fuck is Bruce?" I ask, looking Holt in the eyes.

"What did we say about swearing?" says Jones, turning red.

"Seems your friends have abandoned you, *man,"* says Roberts. Holt turns his watch on his wrist, then decides to take it off and lay it on the table. There's an aerial photograph of the Eyre Peninsula on the wall.

"We're going to play a little game," says Holt. "It's called hide the hippy." He takes his badge off and puts it next to his watch. He takes the gun in his freckled hand, flings the chamber out and removes the bullets. He puts the bullets in his top pocket. I look him straight in the eyes. They are dead.

"Look," I say, "I didn't mean it. I'll do anything you want, you name it." Roberts laughs.

"I'm not cleaning the mess up this time," says the big guy. His voice vibrates through his hands that clasp my shoulders.

"You'll do as you're told, Paul," says Holt. He's putting one bullet back in the chamber. The weapon is black and oozes black. Holt opens the chamber again and shows me one bullet in there, the end is gold. He flicks the cylinder with his finger and looks up at the ceiling. He takes a deep breath and closes the chamber without looking. He stands up. "Put him up against the wall," he says. The big guy lifts the chair by the arms and throws me and the chair against the wall. He grabs my collar and pulls me up, choking me. One of them punches me in the stomach and I fall back in the chair and can't get air. I'm gasping. Sweat is pouring out of my palms. Holt grabs me by the throat and slams my head against the wall, his silver fillings are exposed as he talks.

"*What did we say about swearing*? Everyone has rules to follow, you little prick. We've got men dying in Nam for us and lazy shits like you living off our taxes. The cities are full of you little pricks." The end of his nose is thick, like a big callous. I close my eyes. *The Vietnam guy on the train. He only had one arm. He winked to me.*

"Get stuffed," I say. "I've never been on the dole a day in my life."

"That so? Well, who's the government guy paying all your bills? If he wasn't here, you'd be dead by now."

"Okay, okay, joke's over fellas," I say. "You made your point, can you let me go now?" I try to look them all in the eyes, but they ignore me.

"This is no joke, sonny," says Holt, the muscles around his eyes twitch. He drops off the table, and grabs my cheeks, pulling my lips together. The skin below my eyes hurts. This is getting serious. These guys are evil.

"Ia wahd wop wows?" He lets go of my cheeks.

"What did you say?"

"I fucked up, okay. C'mon guys."

"They're all sorry behind closed doors," says Jones, playing with the envelope opener. *Riverbank. Norman. Monkey.* I've been stupid, I've been a fool. I deserved all I got. Did my time. Kept my nose clean. I don't care. Got a busted marriage, a busted band. I'm not laying down for these pricks.

I say to them, "I didn't say I was sorry." I grip the arm rests tight. "I'm—I'm not sorry." My bum clenches. They all start laughing, but they're faking it. My heart is pounding. I feel sick. Holt lifts the gun up and points it at my face. His hand is shaking. The hollow of the barrel is death. I look away but the big guy turns my head back.

"This is your last chance to say sorry, you little fucking cunt."

"This has gone far eno—" says Roberts.

"Shut the fuck up, John," says Holt, waving the gun to one side. "Move out the way, Paul." He pulls the hammer back. "Look at me," he says. "Look at me or I'LL PULL THE

FUCKING TRIGGER." I open my eyes. Blue carpet, wooden desk, black pants. I look him in the eyes. They're lifeless.

"You don't think I've buried guys like you before? I've lost count of the amount of wogs and boongs with concrete blocks tied to their ankles at the bottom of the Spencer. Eh, Jones?" Jones looks like he's about to vomit. Holt looks at him.

"STOP. STOP. STOP!" I yell. "You fucking evil motherfuckers."

"Oh, for Christ's sake. You lot are a bunch of girls," says Holt. His face turns red. He grimaces, and turns his head slightly and bares his teeth. His arm lowers, the gun is pointing at my chest. He brings his other hand up to steady himself.

Holt shakes his head, shifts the barrel to the side of my face and pulls the trigger. I jump. Just a click.

"Let's go," he says, putting his watch and hat on. They follow him out of the room. I'm breathing so fast. I'm so tense. I look at the palms of my hands. They shake uncontrollably. I hold out my fingers, they're playing a piano. I shake my head, make a fist and run my hand through my hair.

"FUCKING HELL," I yell. *Fuck me, fuck me dead.* I look through all the drawers looking for booze, anything. In the filing cabinet, some port. I scull and scull, nearly finishing the bottle. I spill it down my neck and chest, in my beard. I pick up the picture Holt put his hat on. A guy and his wife on their wedding day, all smiles and sunshine. The frame shakes in my sweaty hand. I start to get my breath back. The urge to drink into the blackness. To wipe myself out. To feel like a ghost, hollow, sick, brittle somehow. I find paper and a pen and start writing the first thing that comes.

I'M A CITY KID THAT SAYS WHAT HE THINKS
NO SKIN OFF MY NOSE
POLICE KICKING ME WHEN I'M DOWN
AND NOBODY KNOWS.
WHY WOULD YOU SHOOT SOMEBODY,

OR EVEN CARRY A GUN?
I AIN'T DOING NOTHING HERE
JUST LEAVE ME ALONE.

The door flies open and a waft of air pushes my face. Bruce hangs on the handle.

"There you are, Ron, I've been looking all over for...You alright mate?" His eyes are soft and I love him.

"The cops threatened to kill me." My eyes water and a big lump grows in my throat.

"Here, drink this," he says, handing me his whisky bottle.

Dry mouth. Dry lips. Dry fingers. Wet, sweaty neck. A plank of sunlight crosses the bus, shines on my face. Beer bottles and wine bottles lie about. I woke up cold a few times, but now I'm roasting. A pair of crows chat away in the car park pine tree. I smell bum and feet. I open a few windows that are half covered in dew. My stomach muscles ache. Ralph is asleep in the driver's chair. He smirks. His white socks are turning yellow. He wiggles his toes.

The clock on the dash says nine thirty. Ralph wakes up, startled. He wipes his face, he has little dots of sand in the corners of his eyes.

"Oh, Bon," he looks at the clock. "You're more than a pretty face." He yawns and does a stretch.

"Let's get the fuck out of here," I say. We walk along the main drag looking for the others in the hotel. We sit outside the bakery. I keep a coffee down, but struggle to finish my sausage roll. Our group grows, everyone getting their brains together. The bloke at the hotel says Richard left early.

We clean and load the bus. As we pull out the cops are next to their cars, watching. They follow us out of town. I tell the story of the roulette, but no one believes me. We drive east, fixing the blinds as the sun moves, and join the highway with the road trains, the bare paddocks and cloven hoofs. Warnertown to Redhill, Redhill to Lochiel, Lochiel to Inkerman, Inkerman to Prospect, Prospect to Adelaide. We cross the river on King William Road. A motorbike passes us. I shake my head when I think of the argument Irene and I are going to have. The missing rent. What missing rent? A king wave of all my fuck ups and bitterness swings through my chest. Our marriage feels like a blur of ill-considered commitments. Must resist the urge to line up a list of her fuck ups as a defence. I sip beer, hair of the dog, and bounce in the seat as the bus enters the city.

Ralph drops Bruce, J.B. and me off first, as the others need to go up to Aldgate. I walk up our gravel driveway with my clothes bag banging against my legs. I can't wait to have a shower and a shave and go to the pub for a Sunday roast. The sun is behind the big tree in the back yard and a strange yellow colour is in the air.

"Someone's burning off," says Bruce, cleaning his glasses. On the kitchen table, there are beer bottles, an ashtray with some butts in it and a leather wallet. Bruce opens the wallet, frowning. "Some guy named Pat." His lips curl downward like he doesn't have a clue.

"Your mate, from the bakery," says J.B. I put my bag down in the hallway and start walking towards Irene and my room. Bruce is right behind me. I hear murmuring inside and push the door open. On our bed is Pat and another man with a young girl.

"Oh, that's disgusting," says Bruce. I shut the door and walk back to the kitchen. Who is the girl? Why are they in my room? Lucky Irene isn't here. Bruce checks his room and walks in. We look at each other bewildered.

"What the fuck is that?" he asks. He looks really pissed off.

"I have no idea," I tell him.

"I could tell. When I met him at the bakery that guy was bad news," says Bruce, lighting a cigarette. "Make me one of your special coffees, can you, Bon? I need some cheering up."

I put the kettle on and start wiping the bench. I pour myself a whisky.

"That poor girl," I say.

"Should we go in there?" asks Bruce.

"Sounds like it's finished," I say. The magpies come to the back door, singing. I stir our coffees and top them up with a dram. The liquids separate on the surface. Pat walks in, putting a shirt on. His tall skinny body has no colour. The veins in his arms stick out.

"I needed that," he says, grabbing a fag out of Bruce's packet without asking. Bruce turns to face the other way, then gets up and walks outside. "Where the fuck have you been?" Pat asks me, slapping me on the back.

"We've been half way across the state," I tell him, trying to hide the anger in my voice.

"Listen to this, listen to this," says Pat, bouncing on the tips of his feet. "What do you call a bunch of boongs in a stolen car?" I don't answer. "A car-roberree," he says. He claps his hands. I smile to humour him. The smile disappears from his face. Bruce walks back in.

"Who's the girl?" asks Bruce, who looks like he's about to explode.

"Oh, you wouldn't believe it," says Pat, proud of himself. "We met her at the pub. She said she wanted to meet ya, Mr Bon Scott from Fraternity, so I said I knew ya, and could hook youse two up."

"So you brought her back here?" asks Bruce. I pour another whisky.

"What is this, a trial or something?" asks Pat. "Where else was I gunna bring her? Bon said to pop around anytime. At the bakery. I didn't plan this, we got here and no one was around." He crosses his arms. The front door slaps and then the other guy walks in.

"She gone?" Bruce asks.

"Yep, real young'un that one," the guy says.

"Where does she live?" Bruce is staring at the fake flowers on the table.

"West Beach" says Pat, "You wanna have a go do ya? *Do ya? Eh?*" Bruce turns to him, I've never seen him this angry before. He puts his left hand on his hip, and looks at Pat over the top of his glasses. He speaks slowly, but his teeth show as he speaks.

"No. Fuck wit," he says. "Bon is going to go to her place and take her out to dinner, and apologise."

"This is not my fault," I protest.

"Yeah," says Pat, "why should he? She knew what was happening."

"What?" says Bruce, going bright red and standing up. "That you brought her here under the impression she was going to meet Bon, and then you deceived her and took advantage of her?" Spit flies out of his mouth. I finish my whisky and pour another. "Get out," says Bruce, "Get the fuck out of my house, RIGHT NOW."

Pat looks confused. He turns to his mate, shrugs his shoulders, picks up his wallet, and goes out the back door. The guy follows him. I hear them talking as they walk away. Bruce pours himself a whisky and we finish the bottle. He chain smokes. I'm struggling to focus my vision, getting about as drunk as I hoped.

"You better clean the sheets before Irene gets back," he says.

"Who made you the boss?" I say.

"*Ron*, don't be a pissed off drunk. Just change the sheets before Irene comes back, I won't say--"

"You're as drunk as I am," I say.

"Ron, okay, I've told you before, I don't mind you drinking but don't get aggro."

"Aggro? You're the one yelling and screaming."

"I'm not arguing, Ron, I'm not pissed off with you. Irene will be back in a minute."

"Irene? Fuck Irene, and fuck you too, Bruce." I go outside,

the magpies hop out the way, their heads tilting. I sit on my motorbike and unlock the handlebars. I flick the stand up and reverse it toward the tree. I go to kick start the engine but my foot misses and I fall off and the bike falls on top of me. I laugh on the ground for a while, feeling nothing. I get up and get it started. Bruce is standing in front of me. The centre of the light beam fills his stomach. He grabs the handlebars.

"You're too drunk," he says.

"You gunna fuckin' stop me, are ya?"

"Think of everyone else, Ron."

"Fuck everyone else, no one gives a fuck about me."

"Alright, have it your way," he says. "But I'm not coming to your funeral and I'm not coming to see you in hospital, *you stupid cunt.*" The flash of the kitchen light, the tunnel of the driveway and I'm out into the open road.

Blur. Faster and faster. The bike jerks. Unseen pothole. The engine loud. My helmet on crooked. Seeing double. Double street lights, double white lines. Two curbs. I put one hand over my left eye. Stop at an intersection. The red lights of the car in front swirl and float. Take off. I put my hand back on my eye between gears. The bike revs over and jerks when I release the throttle. I lose balance and fling into the wrong lane.

I correct and pull over to the curb. Hold on to a pole. Look back at the bike lying on the ground, back wheel spinning. *Fucking stand.* I grab the handlebars and lift her up, swing the stand underneath. I sit on the curb. Spit fills my mouth, my head hurts. *Keep swallowing or you'll spew*. Better to walk. Deep breaths. I walk to the middle of the park and lie on my back and look up to the sky. *Fuck them. Fuck 'em all.* I pull my jacket tight. The sleeves always riding up. Spit at the sky. An airplane flashes. I want another drink. Get up. Get up get up get up.

"...He came in three nights ago. Head on collision with a car doing about forty..." Who's that? Hello? Black. I'm floating. Face down. I fly over Adelaide the orange lights circle the wide streets. "...Surgery to stop internal bleeding in the left kidney. Three broken ribs. A broken collar bone... "I fall. I lower. As I lower the sun comes out. I go through the earth to an underground cave. A cool, calm lake. There are emus standing in the water. Their necks droop and drink. One of them has Mum's face. I take my clothes off and dive in the water. I stand up on the sand. I'm alone.

Tyre marks circle and shoot off in the distance. In every direction, only the horizon. Some small shrubs. The sun beating. I pick up a dry chunk of mud left by the single track-marks of a motorcycle.

"Ronald, Ronald, can you hear me, Ronald? I'm going to take your pulse and take a blood sample." The high pitched tapping of curtains being pulled back. I can't see her, but I can feel mother in the room. Breathing machines beeping, a large pipe in my throat. Perforated white sheeting in the ceiling, square pattern repeated. Perforated white blankets pulled tight, like a strait jacket. A television, turned off, suspended from a rail. A bag of chocolate milk drips.

J.B. and me in his ute. My yellow motorbike strapped in the tray. Clutch the dog sitting between us. His pink tongue, his stinky breath. I hand John a tab of acid and take one myself. The beach is long and compact. Tufts of grass in the dunes. J.B. jumps on the back. I start the engine, choose a spot on the far away beach and go as fast as possible only focusing on the one spot. A small river mouth up ahead but I don't slow, I try to go faster and faster whooshing in my ears as loud as the engine. Sand flying up. Splash in the water and I try to break through the river mouth. The stream yellow at the edge and brown in the middle. I go faster and faster and J.B. screams behind. I pick a spot to try to jump the dunes. The bike jerks beneath me. I fly out of the seat. Acid peaking, all warped. I catch the lip of the dune. The sand collapses. I roll into the water, banging my thigh, mouth full of sand and water. J.B. and the motorbike back there, back wheel spinning, sand circles.

Sleep. Awake, sleep. A pigeon smacks into the window. Vacuum cleaner noise. Orderlies and nurses chatting. Like two boobs my feet poke up under the blanket.

"He moved about an hour ago. But his eyes didn't open." Irene. Talking to a nurse. Her soft hand in mine. Her voice like a drug. I give in. I fart and keep my eyes closed.

"Ron, Ron, darling, wake up. Come on now, it's me, Irene. Can you squeeze my hand?" I squeeze her hand. No strength. My skin sags. Numbness tingles up my arm. Fear. Fear is all I feel.

"We nearly lost you Bonnie," she sobs. A tissue in her half-fist. "We nearly lost you, a few times." She sits sideways on the bed. Her hair is tied back. On the chair her handbag and a notebook with some drawings.

"What happened?" I ask.

"You went out into the other lane, straight into a car. You've been here for a week. You left all your teeth on the road." She smiles through her tears. The gap between her two front teeth.

"I'm sorry," I say. I mean it. "You're so beautiful. So beautiful, Irene." Salty tears stream into my mouth.

"Your hands are so cold, they're shaking. Your mum and I have been taking turns, she comes in when I'm at work. She's knitting me a jumper. She's so nice."

"My dad here?"

"No. Just your mum. She says you have to go back to Freo when you get a little better. But you can stay with me, if you want."

"I thought you wanted a divorce?" I ask.

"I'm still angry with you, you pain in the arse. C'mon now, sit up, the nurses said you have to eat lots." She helps with the pillows and pulls the eating trolley over the bed. A red mash with water on top sits in a metal bowl. Irene stirs it. She has our wedding ring on. "C'mon, open up." I shake my head. "*Open, Bon*," she says. She loads my mouth up and I try to swallow but mostly the goo slides down my throat. I try to say I don't want any, but my mouth is too full. "Try not to speak, Ron," she says. "One blink yes, two blinks no. Now, I've been thinking. I found a place in Prospect, a little three bedroom bungalow. It has a nice big kitchen and a bath. It's got gas hot water too, so no more lighting fires for you. What do you think, Ron?" I nod. A nurse pokes her head in.

"Everything all right in here?"

"Yes, thank you," says Irene, twisting. The muscles in her neck make a line up to her jaw. "You remember when we came back on the plane, Bon? When we mucked around in the loo while everyone was asleep?" I nod again, trying to swallow. My arms are trapped under the blanket. "We had a quicky, the first one in ages. Remember? You got me preggers, Bon. I'm three months already. It's due in March." I try to spit the goo out. She shovels another spoonful in. I turn my head away, a burp wells up in my mouth and exits my nose. I turn to her. She opens her eyes wide and looks at me, consoling. I blink twice. "I know, it was a surprise for me too, Bon, best to accept these things. Now. Things are going to change. You're going to have to work and I'll stay home with the kids." Two blinks. She tightens the blankets over my chest. Two blinks. "The doctors say you'll be here another few weeks and then you can move in with me and start working on the house." Two blinks.

Over Irene's shoulder Mum pushes through the curtain and stands behind the bed end. She kisses Irene. She comes over to me but doesn't kiss me, saying, "Nobody would want tae kiss that. Ye've got a right mess ay yerself, haven't ye?" She wears a cardigan and light brown pants. Her hair is greyer. Two knitting needles poke out of her handbag. "What, Ron, ye like...like ye seen a ghost."

"Isa," says Irene, "I was telling Ron about our little surprise."

"Oh, Ron, ye'll be soon playin' with wee kids. Ye can kiss ye old life cheerio then now, eh?" I look at them both, a feeling of terror comes over me. "Oh aye, Ron, ye won't sleep for years. Think of all the misery ye've put me thru." I try to speak. "Try not tae speak too much hen," says Mum. "The pipe they've got in yer throat will ruin yer voice." Irene and Mum look at each other, they raise their eyebrows and then they both start bursting out with laughter. "Hey, Ron, ye really thought Irene was pregnant? Ye poor thing. Ye looked like ye were about tae die." They stand around feeling happy with themselves, playing me for a fool. They must have too much time on their hands.

I fall asleep and wake up to see Mum sitting next to me, beneath the window.

"Oh, Ron." She stands up and keeps knitting as she's chatting. "I've been trying tae keep them quiet, but it's no use. No use at aw. Yer father is relieved Ron. Yer goin' tae be okay. He said tae tell ye South Fremantle are in the grand final."

"Yes, mum."

"Ah don't know why yer breakin' up with Irene. She cares a stoatin deal fer ye, ye know. An don't ye forget it. She's much better than that other girl, the snob."

"Suzy's not a snob, Mum, she's Dutch."

"Don't ye get all worked up now, ye need to rest."

"I'm sorry, Mum."

"Wha?...oh..." She tugs at the wool. "As long as you're alive. Ye've bin goin through gallons ay this chocolate milk. Ah didn't know ye liked it so —"

"I can't taste it, Mum, goes straight in my stomach."

"Bruce should be comin in th-day."

"Thought he said he wasn't going to?"

"He did say that. I've bin staying at his mother's. I told him he better think twice about not visitin'." Some ravens fly by. "Bruce says his mum and me are exactly th' same, but we look nothing like each other." A deep voice rumbles through the curtains. Bruce's voice. He's wearing a black leather jacket, jeans and R.M. Williams boots. His boots tap on the vinyl floor.

"Speak ay th' devil," says Mum. Bruce looks at me and looks shocked. "We were just talkin' about ye, how ye said ye ma and me are exactly th' same." I manage a smile. He nods.

"No, Isa," says Bruce, all serious, "You and my Mum don't look the same, you *are* the same."

"What's 'at supposed tae mean?" says Mum, offended.

"You both nag the shit out of us," I say. Mum shakes her head in embarrassment and Bruce's face goes all red and then he starts laughing and I join in but the pipe gets stuck in my throat and I start coughing and thrashing in the bed kicking the blankets off. Mum sits me up and pats me on the back and then rubs. I feel hopeless.

"We might nag you, but until ye can look after yourselves, I guess we'll have tae," she says. Bruce takes some *Phantom* comics out of a paper bag and gives them to me. "Yoelistenin' tae me, ye two?" Mum says, pointing at us. "Us mothers spend our whole lives trying tae keep ye boys safe, an' we're the ones that have to pick up th' pieces."

"Mum!" I say.

"Come back to Fremantle, Ron," she says. "Forgot abou' this music business an' bide a normal life with ye father an' Dereck and Graeme. Ye can still play in the pipe band with ye father. He still enjoys it ye know." She gives Bruce and I long stares. Bruce starts flicking through a comic that's resting on one of his crossed legs.

"Oh, ye boys never listen tae me anyway, what's the use?" She packs up her things.

"Where are you going, Mum?"

"If ye have to know, I'm going tae th' bathroom. Ronald, Bruce can take care of ye."

Bruce starts playing with the television controls above the bed, his belly hanging out beneath his shirt. The TV is up on a frame. A white spot grows in the centre of the screen.

"Jeez, you get the royal treatment here, don't ya?" he says, sitting down. The sound comes out a little speaker above the bed. Bruce grabs a bowl of fruit off the table. I look out the window, not a cloud in the sky.

"Oh for fuck's sakes," says Bruce, pointing at the screen, "remember this cunt? Ian Meldrum. Remember when we were filming *Seasons of Change* at Channel Nine and he was a dancer?"

"Yeah, I remember." My voice sounds like someone else. "He punched one of the girls out." I try to sit up, but I'm too weak. "I'll never forget at some music festival, after we got back from England, he completely ignored me. I went to say hello..."

"How does he go from dancer to show host? That's what gets me. I tell ya, the nepotism and corruption in this country blows my mind, man." He shakes his head. "He couldn't dance in the first place." Bruce rejigs my pillow.

"Bruce," I say, the heart machine beeping quicker, "I'm sorry, Bruce."

"Don't worry about it," he says. "You're the one stuck in hospital. You've got some beauty bruises. Your skin's all see through..."

"I shouldn't be here. *You warned me*."

"I wasn't gunna come."

"Why did you?" I ask.

"My mother told me to."

"When I've got nothing to do I go mental."

"David-fucking-Bowie," he says, standing up and getting closer to the screen. "I've been watching a lot of these music films lately, Ron, trying to figure out where we went wrong..."

"I don't care anymore, Bruce."

"What the fuck are you talking about Ron? Look at him. See? He stares straight into the camera. *If* you can call *him* a he."

"The music. Making it. All that shit. I don't care anymore."

"You gotta talk directly to the audience. None of this being aloof. See he hardly ever uses words that end in 'I.N.G.'?"

"I'm going back to Fremantle," I say.

"Use images and combine them with the story. You have to look clean and sharp. All the words have to have meaning, none of this *la la la* shit."

"You listening, Bruce?"

"What?" He turns to look at me. He turns back. "Every song has to have a melody and a chorus."

"Bruce?"

"What, Ron?" he says, annoyed.

"I haven't got the energy anymore." He throws his head back and laughs. He looks out the window, cleans his nails, using his facial hair.

"You're just a bit banged up, Ron. You'll be right as rain soon. What else are you gunna do? You stupid bastard. You're no good at anything but singing."

"I'll find something, was thinking about crayfishing again."

"Yeah, right."

"There's good money..."

"You may as well go back to the fertiliser factory," says Bruce. "Your problem is you're one extreme or the other. You'll be better in a few months. Don't kill yourself in the meantime. Bands break up. Shit happens. People get kicked out, they get replaced. You keep your eyes on the prize, Ron."

A walking stick pokes through the divider curtain and the man in the next bed asks us to keep quiet.

"Anne says hello, sends her love," says Bruce, throwing a comic on the bed.

"You two going alright?"

"Yeah, we're okay," he says, shrugging his shoulders.

"Hey, Bruce, remember when we worked in the hotel in London?"

"Yeah, course I do." He frowns, pushes his glasses back up his nose.

"Remember some mornings, I'd wake you up and wait for

you outside? Out the front?

"Mmmm."

"Remember the little window in your bedroom?" His eyes open wide, and a big grin comes over his face.

"You bloody pervert," he says, laughing. "Oh jeez, I always wondered why you had that stupid smile on your face, I thought it was the hash."

AC/DC
MELBOURNE – 1975

GOOD EVENING IRENE,

HOW YOU DOIN SPUNK? IN MELBOURNE BUILDING THE BAND UP, WE'RE PLAYING ABOUT 8 OR 9 SHOWS A WEEK. GOT A SHOW AT MYERS TODAY AND AT THE HARD ROCK CAFE LATER TONIGHT. OUR NEW MANAGER BROWNING RUNS THE CAFE SO WE CAN PLAY THERE ANYTIME WE WANT.

REMEMBER THE FASHION DESIGNER, KATE, IN ST KILDA? RAN INTO HER ~~THE~~ YESTERDAY AND SHE STARTED GOING ON ABOUT WHAT A SHAME WE BROKE UP AND HOW LOVELY A COUPLE WE WERE AND SO ON. SHE GOT ME THINKING HARD ABOUT HOW I MISS YOU AND HOW I COULD HAVE DONE THINGS DIFFERENTLY.

GRAEME'S IN TOWN SO HOPEFULLY HE CAN FILL ME IN WITH ALL THE DETAILS. HE SAID HE RAN INTO YOU IN ADELAIDE. I'LL SEND YOU THE FIFTY BUCKS I OWE YOU AS SOON AS POSSIBLE. THERE'S A CHANCE WE'LL BE OVER BEFORE WE

HEAD TO LONDON, BUT IF NOT I'LL TELEGRAPH YOU THE FORWARDING ADDRESS. GOTTA GO. LOTS OF LOVE.

BON

"Bon, Bon, come quick," says Judy, this root rat I've been seeing since I arrived in Melbourne. Was good to begin with, but I think I've started something I don't have the balls to finish. I'm listening to the possums scratch in the roof, jotting some lines for a song about hitch-hiking. "Bon, come on, get up, John Lee broke up with Kate, the bastard. She's all messed up, get out here. *Now.*" I slip a silk robe on and walk into the kitchen, my feet patter on the floor. Angus and Malcolm's cigarette smoke layers fill the room. Ralph, our spider, has a blanket over his shoulders. They all have a cup of tea and hand of cards. Angus is nearly naked and his guitar is between him and the table. I open my robe and flash everyone to say hello. Kate's sobbing, her make up dribbling, eyes red, like the colour of her hair.

"You can do better than that bastard anyway," says Judy.

"What happened, Kate?" I ask.

"We were at the Sapphire Rock," she's short of breath, "having a good time. I don't know, maybe someone spiked my drink, and when I come back from the toilet, he's kissing this other woman."

"Fast worker," adds Angus, throwing down three of a kind. "Whatya got?"

"Did you go up to him?" I say. Judy is stroking her hair.

"No," says Kate, "I had to leave, I got to Landsdowne Road and thought I'd see if the light was on." The AC/DC party house, Landsdowne Road. Big enough to sleep forty people.

"C'mon, we'll set you up in the lounge room," I say.

Back in the blanket in my own bed, I slide my hand up and grab some boob. Judy puts her hand over mine to stop me. The light outside has gone from black to bruise. I yawn. Her skin is nice and soft.

"Why are all men such fucking pricks?" says Judy, her voice muffled in the pillow. Her hair tickles my face. "Do you even give a shit, Bon?"

I take her bait. "They weren't suited for each other. She'll find someone else," I say.

"She'll find someone else," she says, wriggling out of my arms. "Is that all you have to say? You probably think about moving on to the next girl as soon you fuck them, you selfish idiot."

"I never said that."

"That's why you got divorced, isn't it? Couldn't keep your dick in your pants?" I fist the blanket up over my face, she pulls it back.

"No," I say. "We fell apart in London, *Fraternity* fell apart, then I had the motorbike accident. You don't know me from a bar of soap, so don't start—"

"No. No. No. I don't," she says, her pale face squaring up with mine. "You think you're some big shot, that's all I know. You never tell me anything. Yesterday you said you loved me, and now the boys tell me you're going overseas. When were you going to let me in on this big secret?" I can tell you, she's not doing herself any favours carrying on like this. The possums start fighting in the roof as well. Must be the full moon.

"You know the band is going all the way," I say. "I said when—"

"All the way to the ego farm," she says, standing up now. Her hips poke out. "Get over yourself, you fucking idiot. You're just another band. AC-fucking-DC. Woop-de-doo. It's a bloody faggot's name. Angus dresses up as a school boy, for Christ's sake. The only reason why anyone takes any notice is because their brother was in the *Easybeats*."

"Who told you that?" I ask, about to blow my top.

"Everyone knows, dipshit."

"Well, yeah, you're just a stupid junkie. What would you know?" Her arms akimbo. Her thighs bare.

"You're on the shit too. What are you, some kind of angel?"

I've had it a few times. Overdosed once. Too much for my little body. She starts packing her bag. Her bum jolts, hair flying from side to side.

"I promised your sister I'd come to her party."

"You're such a retard, Bon. You come to the party and you see what happens." She grabs her keys off the dresser, puts her heels on, and slams the door. I try to sleep but my heart's racing. I grab my notebook.

OH HONEY, YOU'RE ALWAYS SMILING
OH ~~HONEY~~ BABY, YOU'VE GOT ~~SERIOUS~~
SOME SERIOUS STYLING
WHEN YOU WALK OUT THE DOOR ~~ONCE MORE~~
LIKE A GLACIER YOU THAW
YOU'VE BEEN LEAVING FOR TWO MONTHS
I KNOW I'M A REAL ~~CUNT~~ NICE GUY
HANGING AROUND LIKE A FLY
HANG AROUND BABY, JUST HANG AROUND.

The brothers tune their guitars. A red Gibson SG and a red Gretsch. Their instruments are nearly as big as they are. Their hair covers their eyes. They don't speak. They slash where the pick guards would be. Their feet tap, the lino snaps, their fingers fly, flick and hammer.

There's uncut strings at the machine heads. There's dishes piling up on their bed heads, but they don't notice. Ashtrays, coasters, dirty magazines. Loose change, bottles of milk, shoes on the floor, the heater on full bore. Their guitars twang, and you can make out the tune, they're working on a song based on a TV cartoon. They bend and squeal, restructure and steal. With some messing, their sick harmonics find a cure.

This train ain't stopping. This service is express. I lay my body over the tracks, let the riffs roll back, and they kick me, they push me faster and faster. They let me see further than before. No marriage, no babies, none of that. They string you up, string you out, let me show them evil ways. I'll change my spots when I change my jeans, ya know. They lock on a groove and hold it there for a bit. I see fire and the words these sounds demand. I feel work in their play. My celebrations are a revolt. My laughing images suffer. My time is overdue. They've thrown their watches in the bin.

"Fuckin' hell, Angus, your breath stinks," says Malcolm. "When's the last time you brushed your teeth?" He speaks as if uttering is a chore, and everyone should know what he's thinking because it makes perfect sense to him.

"I dunno, Malc," says Angus, wearing his guitar and undies. "I'm going to the deli, you want anything?"

"You gunna do the dishes even once this week?" asks Malcolm, holding a broom. Angus' shoulders slump. He was having a good day until now.

"Do you want anything from the shop, Malc?"

"Just fags. And git me a chocolate milkshake."

"I'm not getting you a choclo, Malc, git your own," says Angus. "You want anything, Bon?" He wipes his nose with the back of his hand. He has enough energy to power a small town.

"Can you grab some bread, the newspaper, and some rollie papers please, Angus? There's some money on my dresser." I put the kettle on and start filling the sink. The front fly-wire door snaps. We're nearly out of dishwashing detergent. Malcolm puts some Muddy Waters on. Michael Browning, our manager walks in. We call him Browning. He looks more like a furniture removalist, or rugby player, than a band manager. He sits at the table with his back to the wall, lights a fag and starts playing with the ashtray, swirling it. He has a large forehead and deep set eyes. His dark hair is thin on top.

"Ever heard of knocking?" asks Malcolm, lighting a cigarette.

"Nice to see you too, Malc. Look, I need you boys to do an interview today, between the show at Myers and the Hard Rock gig.

"Oh yeah, who with?" I ask.

"Molly Meldrum." Molly and I go back to *The Valentines* days.

"Molly! The poof," says Malcolm.

"Hey," I say, "don't criticise someone of the likes of Ian Molly Meldrum. He's very important in Australia, and can pull a few strings or two. And a few dicks, might I add." I give them a cheeky smile. "He's a real down-hill skier."

Browning chuckles, and lights another cigarette. I open the window. "Moving right along," he says. "The show at Myers is for an hour. Should be a breeze. Then you'll meet Molly at three. It's not live, so don't worry. Paul Drane will be there, he wants to talk about the *Long Way to the Top* film clip.

"Who's he?"

"He's the director at the A.B.C.," says Browning. "Phil's going to pick you all up, and you can meet at the cafe afterwards." I see myself working up the crowd, provoking them with gonorrhoea talk. I flick the switch and become *Bon, the Rock Star.* With these guys, the thought of going for it isn't the same as before. It's for real.

FROM THE FIRST DAY TO THE LAST DAY AT SCHOOL
I KNEW THAT I WANTED TO SING
NO ONE KNEW OR UNDERSTOOD
~~NO ONE~~ NOBODY WANTED TO KNOW

MUM AND DAD THEY SCRATCH THEIR HEADS
THOUGHT ~~WAS ALL FOR SHOW~~ I WAS WASTING TIME
GUNNA BE THE BEST SOME DAY
GUNNA RULE THE ROOST, YOU'LL SEE

~~GOING~~ GUNNA TO BE A FIRST CLASS SINGER
GUNNA BE A FIRST CLASS STAR

"What's the latest on England, then?" asks Malcolm.

"Basically," Browning's voice is soft and low, the opposite of Malcolm's, "Atlantic are not going to pay, they're happy to pay for publishing and distribution, but we're on our own for the first tour."

"Fucking tight arses," Malcolm spits. "That mean we keep the profits from the shows?"

"There won't be any," says Browning. "First few tours always run at a loss. You've seen what happens when we go to places like Geraldton and Katanning."

"Well, we'll be keeping an eye on the books." Browning's head tilts, I see he's hiding his disappointment. Malcolm doesn't trust him.

"Have you got new material?" Browning fires back. I finally get this frying pan clean and place it on the drying rack. Malcolm, insulted by Browning's question, is about to reply when in walks Angus. He's holding a paper bag with bread, milk and newspapers. A milkshake in one hand, the straw in his mouth, another milkshake tucked between his elbow and torso. His guitar hangs loosely over his body.

"Old duck at the shop says she won't serve me anymore, unless I wear clothes," he says, sliding the bag onto the bench.

"I'm talking to Alberts and the bank," says Browning, wiping smoke from his eyes. "I think we can roll it, but we need to do some bigger shows in Melbourne and Sydney first. *Back Street Crawler* sound pretty positive we can tour with them, although we're talking to Ritchie Blackmore as well."

"Webe read," says Malcolm, drinking his milkshake.

"What?" says Browning.

"We're ready," says Malcolm.

"Okay, so we're all set. Between now and then as many shows as possible, and recording whenever we're in Sydney," says Browning. "Be nice to Molly."

"We got an interview with Molly?" asks Angus.

"Molly, the poof," repeats Malcolm. Angus laughs, half goat, half pig. Angus starts brainstorming.

"Yeah, sausage roll festival, Mt Bulla mate. Umm, rear view Wagga Wagga. Wheelbarrow racer."

"Iron Knob Alpine climber," I add, encouraging him. He's

salivating.
"Mount Bogong. Bacchus Marsh, mate."

A yellow station wagon belts up the street, cuts the driveway and digs two deep track marks in the grass. Phil and Mark, drummer and bass player. Angus, Malcolm and I jump in. "Nice hair, Bon," says Phil. I'm wearing black leather pants, a leopard print vest, and my most comfortable ladies boots.

"Mark, this is Bon, our singer," Malcolm says. I swing around, awkward, and offer my hand to shake his. He's stockier than the rest of us. His hands are soft and a little fleshy. All these guys are about seven years younger than me. They make me feel twenty one again.

"Who'd you steal this car off?" I ask Phil. He has a skeleton key to almost any car. His father is a used car salesman.

"Borrowed it from a mate," he says, turning to me, smiling.

"Where are we off to then, fellas?" asks Mark, happy and enthusiastic. Malcolm and Angus keep smoking and looking out the window, just another day. Once I realise they're not answering I pipe up.

"Myers. Hope you got a good belt on."

"What for?"

"To keep your clothes on..."

"FUCKIN' watch where you're going, DICK-HEAD," yells Phil, releasing the steering wheel, letting the car straighten itself.

GOING TO A MATINÉE, PLAYIN HEAPS OF SHOWS
WEAVING ~~THROUGH~~ IN THE TRAFFIC, PLAYING IN A BLOW
TAKING RISKS, LOOKIN GOOD, RUNNING
HIGH, RUNNING LOW
WHEN YOU'RE FAST, YOU'RE ~~ALWAYS MISUN-
DERSTOOD??~~ HIGH UP IN THE HOOD.

We cross the bridge near the art gallery and wait at the lights near Flinders Station. Hundreds of people criss-cross and then trams clack-clack by and we weave up the mall and take an alley to the back of the department store. There's young kids everywhere. AC-fucking-DC. Pat and Ralph are unloading the vans. I got those fellas the job from the old *Fraternity* days. I go to help but Ralph tells me to bugger off.

In the staff lunch room we sit around a large table. A fridge and bench line one wall, a sink another. There's a blackboard with all these mottos. On the table a tray with some biscuits and cheese and crackers. Angus taps on his guitar. Malcolm is giving Mark the low down on what'll happen. We're only playing for half an hour, so it's not a big deal. Angus opens his gig bag. A terrible stench floats out, like a bunch of bananas left in a school bag over summer holidays.

Malcolm says, "Jes-fuckin-christ, Angus. That's awful, take it outside. You even air it after last night?" By the end of the show Angus was a hot flannel.

In walks Browning, his nose starts twitching. "It's chaos out there, lads. There's girls everywhere, the ads must have worked. I've never seen anything like this. There must be about seven thousand of them. They've scared all the boys away. Most of the floors are trashed. The fire brigade are on stand-by."

"We're playing though, aren't we?" asks Malcolm. Angus is shaking his shirt, sniffing it.

"Security are at the front of the stage," says Browning.

Mark says, "Well, they won't go anywhere near Angus the way he smells." No one laughs. Malcolm looks at Mark like he's just slept with his sister. Angus puts his school satchel on. Phil's tapping his sticks on his legs.

"Listen up, guys," says Browning. "Half an hour and we're out of here. The store manager only really wants us to play *TNT*." He is nervous. He's making me nervous. *What damage can a bunch of screaming girls do?*

"One more thing," says Browning, jumping backwards onto the bench, kicking the cupboards with his heels. "We're off to London!" Mark and Phil are all smiles. I have an inner smile.

Malcolm, now with his guitar on, waits for silence.

"Why didn't you tell us this morning?" he asks.

"I didn't know then, only found out this afternoon, they're ten hours behind you know?" says Browning. His legs stop swinging. "I wanted to tell you all together." He shakes his head and mumbles something to himself. Band politics. Best to stay out of it, ya know. In walks Pat, all cheery, half his front teeth missing. His nose twitches and he's about a foot taller than Angus, messing up the little fella's hair. He pauses. Rubs his hands. He cannot contain his excitement.

"Did you horse and cart, Angus?" he says. Mark laughs loudly. "I was thinking about you the other day, what was it? Oh, yeah. I was watching this porno and this chick was playing a guitar, you woulda loved it."

"Oh yeah?" says Angus, looking up.

"Don't you worry, you little cunts, I'll look after you," says Pat. "Now, let's ROCK AND ROLL."

One by one we walk up. Angus is jumping, his satchel bounces on his back. Mark looks pale, taking deep breaths. I finish my bourbon and throw the cup in the bin. Phil sits down and tightens the snare springs. Girls scream and bounce and pull their hair. Some are crying. They've made t-shirts with our names in texta. They're wearing black eye liner. Some look happy, some sad. Toilet paper rolls fly.

Security have their arms linked and try to hold the rush back. I grab the microphone from the front of the stage. Mannequin limbs fall at my feet. Bodies rush forward. I introduce us but I can't be heard over the screaming. Phil counts us in, Malcolm and Angus strike the opening chord. I see Ralph at the side of the stage, his eyebrows raised. He's struck by a girl who's rushed around the guards. Angus goes up to a microphone and starts "OI. OI. OI." They scream louder. I can hardly hear the band. I start singing, *You see me ride out on the sunset*, and another wave tests the security link. There's nowhere to move.

Mark is shitting himself. A dummy head smacks one of the guards in the face. He checks his forehead, letting the arm link go and with another wave of pressure the stage is stormed, girls grabbing my arms and clothes. The music stops and you can hear the rumble of the guitars getting scratched.

I head for the staff room and go out the fire exit and in the stairwell is Angus. We jump whole flights and break out into the daylight, into the alleyway stink. "We better keep running," I tell him and I start away from the mall, dodging puddles. We come out onto the street and there's a whole bunch of them and I'm getting puffed out. One of the girls sees us and yells so we run toward Elizabeth Street Markets. There's a tram stopped and we jump on. We buy a ticket from the inspector, sweating like buggery. But the tram doesn't move. Next thing the tram is surrounded and the driver opens the doors and they rush in.

"Okay ladies," says Angus, his guitar still on. "One at a time, one at a time. Watch the guitar." Most of the people on the tram look horrified.

Small streams gush inside blue-stone curbs. Drizzle blurs headlights. Black figures hop and step from shelters to trams to keep their feet dry. A bunch of football fans dressed in black and white sing their theme song. We stand and sway holding onto a pole.

We get off and find a row of workers' cottages. Judy said not to come, but she'll get over it and I promised Christine. A group hangs out in the front yard, some of them using a vine as a chair. On the verandah, a long red vinyl couch. Four women sit with their legs crossed, their stockings different colours. Their heavily made up faces flash by the fire in the drum. Raindrops hiss. *Ladies*. They giggle at Angus.

The hallway is packed so we head straight for the back, cellophane over the lights. The stereo up. No sign of Judy or Christine. We stand against the wall in the kitchen and I take a swig of whisky. Angus has a swig. "Okay, Angus, I'm gunna do the human kangaroo. You watch the master at work." He sniggers and ash falls on the carpet. I figure I can get naked out the back and do the kangaroo through the house then circle around the alley and jump the fence at the back and put my clothes back on. I open a door and inside there's three guys and a girl sitting around with spoons, syringes, bags of white powder and a couple of jelly rubbers. A girl is asleep on a bean bag in the corner. There's a line for the toilet so I find my way up the back and into the car shed. I put all my clothes and shoes on the front seat of the open car. I tuck my lolly bag and old fella between my legs, grab a handful of grass, bring the outside of my thumbs together, tuck my elbows and knees together, and start hopping toward the house. All the girls waiting for the toilet give out screams and laughter. In the kitchen I put some grass in my mouth and chew from side to side. Angus goes blood red in embarrassment. Most of the blokes are unimpressed.

Bounce into the lounge room and some bird grabs my bum. Hop up the hallway, people happily clear the way. I throw my grass in the fire and warm up a bit. I run around the back and jump the fence and open the shed and get dressed. I go to a quiet spot by the back fence and chuck a piss. The grass is wet and squeaks and comes up above my boots. Pitch black with the party music circling. *Don't drink too fast.* At least I'm pissing and not spewing.

I re-enter the party. In the hallway everyone's gathered around, the dancing has stopped and, being a short arse, I can hardly see over everyone's shoulders. "It's your mate," a bloke says. "You better get in there." I push people out the way. In the centre of the circle is Angus, stark-bloody-naked, except his guitar over his lolly bag.

"Givme clothes back," he's yelling. Some tall skinny guy in a flannel shirt. Angus is steaming and spitting like a dog with rabies. The guy holds him on the forehead.

"I haven't got your clothes, little fella." Someone pinches Angus' bum and he thrusts himself forward and starts having a go at everyone.

"Okay everyone, alright, show's over." I grab Angus under the arms, the head of his guitar stabbing people.

And then I hear, "Yes, show is over Bon." It's Judy and she's poking me in the neck. "I told you not to come here, now you and Angus, piss off." Her puffy fringe bounces and I find it hard to take her seriously.

"Where's Christine?"

"I told you to fuck off," she says, pushing me out the front gate, me holding Angus.

"What happened to your clothes, Angus?"

"They were in the laundry. I did the human kangaroo and when I went to get dressed someone'd nicked them." I feel bad and responsible so I take my pants off and give them to him. We walk to the main road looking for a taxi. All the restaurants and cafes are pretty full so we wait on the outskirts for a while. A big brown Ford drives by and then about a minute later drives by again and this time someone's leaning out the rear window yelling, *Go home you faggots*. I start doing stretches and star jumps to make it seem like I'm supposed to be half naked. Angus has his arms crossed and he's not happy and he asks me not to tell anyone.

A taxi finally comes and slows down, but when he sees us he drives off. I'm about to give up hope and start walking to the tram stop when a little blue Datsun pulls up and the driver leans over and winds the window down. He's got a cowboy hat on.

"You fellas in a tight spot?"

Angus jumps in the front and I jump in the back with the dog and swag. We start driving along Smith Street the bright lights off to our right, quick whisky shot.

"Where yas off to?"

"Goin' to the city," I say, "to the Hard Rock cafe."

"No worries, boss, whatchya doin' there?"

"Playing a show," says Angus. "We can get you in if you want."

"No, that's okay boss, they won't let me in with a dog."

"We can get you in, easy, our manager is the owner."

"What, you fellas playing *tonight?*"

"Yeah."

"What's the name of your band?"

"AC/DC."

"Never heard of yas," he says.

The Hard Rock cafe, a large refurbished Georgian joint. Everything is wood, except the half Cadillac above the bar. Framed copies of famous gold and platinum records line the walls. Downstairs there's a whole floor filled with pinball machines. The place is pumping. Must be because of the publicity from the Myers show. Ralph is beavering away on stage. His long blonde hair keeps falling in his face, but he never ties it back. We get a good sound in here because of the intimacy. There isn't really a stage, just a small step and some mikes. Angus and I go out the back. Malcolm, Phil and Mark are sitting around a small coffee table, eating burgers. Angus finds his gig bag and gets dressed and gives my pants back.

"You boys forgot about the interview," says Malcolm. "We arranged the film clip without you."

"Oh yeah," I say, grabbing a chip. "What are we doing?"

"A float down Swanston Street, like *Brown Sugar* in New York."

"With bagpipes?"

"Yeah, we organised for some Scottish bagpipe players to join us."

"When are we on?" I ask him.

"Five minutes," he says, "The support pulled out."

"What's first?" asks Mark. His pudgy face looks annoyed.

"*Live Wire*," says Malcolm, sculling his beer.

Malcolm and Phil and Mark walk out together. There are minor cheers. Then Angus walks out and starts provoking everyone with his devil horn gestures, his tongue poked out, his legs like elastic bands. I'll wait until just before the first verse before going out, sneaking in a few more shots of whisky. Mark begins the first brooding note, over and over. The volume and presence rises. Malcolm turns his volume up and his guitar squeals before he palm mutes. I run out when Malcolm starts strumming the three chords. Get ready for lift off.

A blue spotlight grows stronger and stronger on Angus, who's standing on top of his speaker stack. His leg taps to the beat, his face covered by the school cap. Some people laugh at him. He is all the ridiculous parts of ourselves rolled into one. Phil's cymbals are like gold stepping stones. The bass drum kicks in, big and heavy. Ralph lets the smoke machine go.

Angus jumps off the speaker boxes, light as, and runs into the audience. They part for him and he nearly falls over. His mouth is open and he looks crazy. His guitar lead gets caught on one of the mike stands, but Ralph is on the job. Angus pauses, as if frozen, cranks his volume knob, the amp hums. I scream, "WOOAHH." The boys go full volume. BANG. BANG. The battle has begun. I wrap the lead in my right and grip the mike with my left. I jump out of the way of Angus who is like a caged rat. I flick my hair back and start singing, *If you're looking for trouble*, I open my eyes and stare at a chicky-babe, *I'm the man to see*. I give her a wink.

For the chorus Malc and Mark walk synchronised to the mikes and join me in a call and response. I sing *I'm a Live Wire,* they repeat, *Live Wire*. Camera flashes trap us. When the chorus finishes they return to their spots. Mark and Phil drop out leaving Malc and Angus riffing a Little Richard-type bridge. Once we get warmed up, time flies. When the song finishes I scull two bourbon and Cokes.

High Voltage next. We play the verse and chorus. Time for more call and response. I ease to the front of the stage. "I want you to chant," I say. "I said I want you to chant." I take better grip of the mike lead, tense my body up.

"HIIIGGH."

Crowd: "High."

"I said, HIIIIGHHH." This gets them going. "Okay, come on." Mark is grooving. He's got the body of his bass up on his right thigh. Malcolm comes in licking up, his head jerking. I look at Angus, his mouth open, tongue hanging out. No confusion. Everyone knows where this is headed and the song is going to explode and I'm going to blow. I'm spinning, I'm dancing, this is my time. Angus's guitar growls like a cat fucking. I scream as loud as I can, "I said HIGGH, VOLTAGE, Rock and ROLL, ROLL. ROLLA." The band takes it up another gear, louder still. The room starts swinging. My hearing goes muffled. I fall.

"Bon, Bon. Get up." It's Ralph. Loud guitars and drums.

"Where am I?" I ask.

"You're in heaven, mate. Hear that guitar?"

"Why are you here then, you bastard?"

"You went too hard and passed out. Here, drink this." He holds my head up, I open my mouth. Water. He keeps his hand behind my head. "And again," he says. Bourbon, straight.

"Lansdowne Road please, mate" says Angus to the driver. My head flops on the cold, wet window. White streetlights bring out the fog as they flash by. Shadows pan.

"Where we playing tomorrow?"

"What?"

"Where we playing tomorrow, Angus?"

"Geelong Town Hall."

"That's right, *fucking* Geelong."

"What?"

"Your ears ringing too?"

"Nah, you're slurring a bit," he says. Sounds perfectly normal to me, ya know.

"Sorry, Angus, I get a bit carried away."

"Tha's alright." We cross some track and my head bashes on the window. My plate moving about in my mouth. We drive by a closed pub, people trying to hail us, yelling and carrying on.

"Don't follow me, Angus," I blurt out.

"What the fuck you on about, Bon?"

"Whatever I do, don't follow me, Angus. You got your own way, and getting pissed ain't it. I don't know, I just get carried away, that's all."

"You'll be alright by the morning," he says. "It's not me you have to worry about."

NOW YOU HOLD MY HAIR BACK AS
I'M LOOKIN RATHER SICK
BUT WHAT'S ~~REALLY~~ KINDA FUNNY IS
YOUR FRIENDS THINK I'M A PRICK.
THIS AINT NO LEVEL PLAYING FIELD
THIS GOOD OLD DRINKING RACE
YOUR CHEATING AND YOUR BEATING
WHEN YOU SIT ON MY FACE.

***

Rubbing my forehead to loosen the hangover. Nothing a few aspirin and a couple of coffees won't fix. Mark pokes his head in and tells me there's some big ugly bastard who would like to see me urgently. I tell Mark to tell him to come back in a few hours, but he won't have it. I figure if I go out there in just my shorts he'll scaddadle fast. I squeeze by Malc and Angus playing in the hallway, amps turned low. A bearded bloke, button nose, upside-down V shaped eyebrows, whisky hair. He's wearing a holey black polo shirt, his chest hair bursts out the top.

"I see you got your fighting shorts on," he says. His face snarls. The boys stop playing. He grabs me by the hair and drags me out the front where two of his mates are waiting with their arms crossed, chins up. Too many beers and pies.

"Where's Judy?" he asks, holding my face close to the grass blades. Ah, this is the bit where my screwing around comes back to bite me, ya know.

"Don't know mate," I say. "You're the one always bashing her up." Okay, he's starting to really hurt.

"She tells me you gave her the jack."

"She's lying," I say. "Besides, it's more than you've ever given her." Next thing he's punching me in the face and I'm back-pedalling, trying to protect my face, big rings on his rookers, and he knocks me straight into the rose bush, all the thorns ripping my back and legs like a newspaper. I kinda like his passion. Another hundred needles in my scalp as he picks me up. Into the next bush, an almighty whack to the base of my head on the trunk. I can hardly see but what I can see is his black figure and his gut drooping and he says, "Stay away from my daughter you little fucking dickhead." Off he goes and I spit out my broken dental plate, all bloody. I let my muscles relax and drop deeper into the thorns. Malcolm and Mark arrive to lift me up.

"They smell nice?" asks Ralph.

"You need an ambulance, Bon?"

"I need a dentist and a stiff drink." We get inside and I twist my torso to try get a view of the thorns, pulling them out with tweezers. Bit of a shiner on my eye and a fat lip. In walks Mark to see if I need anything, while the rest of the boys start loading up the bus. He's being all funny hanging about. Then he blurts out, "I think I've got the jack, Bon."

Takes an hour and a half to get to Geelong, stopping at a servo for fuel and Cokes and pies. We go straight to the town hall, a grand old colonial joint with columns and steps fanning out. Ralph and Pat start unloading. I take some pain killers and go for a long walk, circling the outskirts and then cutting back through the mall. Geelong always reminds me of Darc and I at the supermarket and the poor girl I got in trouble with her boss. Bloody Darc and Gabby having a baby soon. The town hall is covered in our posters. In the side entrance Angus and Mark wheel in a black cage.

The hall is long and narrow. High ceiling with wooden slats half-way up the wall. Large square windows are recessed into the white walls. Between the windows a couple of foot long bar heaters blaze red. On the stage, which is about head height, Pat is unrolling some leads. Phil drags a stack of plastic chairs into a storeroom. In the centre of the hall Malcolm and Ralph are chatting to two blokes in cheap navy suits. I sidle up to them.

"—I know, Rob," Ralph's real name is Rob, "but we have to take these threats seriously," says one of the suits. "Is there anybody you can think of who would threaten to kill you? Even as a joke." Ralph looks petrified. Malcolm is getting his angry face.

"Last time we were here," says Ralph, "we had to kick a few punters out, but nothing unusual."

"What about when the cop cuffed you and put you in the back of his car for swearing?" I ask Ralph.

"Oh yeah, there—"

"Who's this?" asks Suit Number One.

"This is Bon, our singer," says Malcolm.

"Got a bit banged up there, son?"

"Just a bit, yeah," I say.

"A cop's not gunna threaten to kill me though, is he?" asks Ralph.

"Not likely. Though, it's not out of the question. Tell you what, here's my card. If anything suspicious happens you ring this number. And if I'm not there, the station will radio us." He grabs his lapels and repositions his shoulder pads. They don't say goodbye, their shoes tap on the floorboards.

"Useless fuckin' drongos," says Malcolm. "Couldn't work their way outa Weeties packet." His face has gone from angry to serious and he stares off out the door.

"It's a joke," says Ralph. "Come on, let's get back to work."

"Where's ya toolbox?" asks Malc. His fists clench. His neck twitches and he stares at some imaginary enemy. His voice gets gruffer, if that's possible. "Where's ya fuckin' toolbox?"

"Beside the stage, on top of one of the amp cases," says Ralph, looking even more terrified. Malcolm storms up to the stage, nearly empties the toolbox, grabs a spanner and three mike stands. He's talking to himself and spitting and his boots bash on the steps and he walks back. Ralph and I look at each other, bewildered. Malc kneels on one leg like he's about to stab one of the stands and dismantles the base. His shoulders heave and his tiny frame struggles. Ralph tries to help but is silenced.

He stands up, hands us a steel rod each and turns and faces the stage, and sticks his fingers in his mouth and lets out a whistle. Not bad, for a little guy. Everyone pauses, except Angus who's sawing one of the bars on the cage.

"Git here," he yells. So there's Phil, our drummer. Mark, the bass player. Pat, the spider, and me and Ralph all standing around in a circle. Angus stands on the stage, sucking on a cig. Brandishing one of his weapons, Malcolm says, "Coupla detectives reckon someone has it in for poor Ralph here." Ralph shrugs his shoulders.

"Don't worry, Malcolm, it's just a joke..." says Ralph.

"Fuck that, we gunna find the fucks," says Malcolm, handing out weapons. Mark, with his Neil Young shirt on, loves this kinda shit. Phil and Pat and Ralph follow. I look back on stage and Angus has disappeared. Outside there's heads in bins, bodies beneath cars, bushes getting poked. Over the road a brown dog sniffs the air. Malcolm and Mark search all the cars along the street. One opens the boot and the other stands ready with bar. A sedan rolls by and they watch it intently.

I'm standing in the sun, starting to feel a little better.

"Oun anon ye," I hear. A hairy black body, short. Big black nose, two rows of white teeth bared. Angus in a gorilla costume.

"What?" I have an inner smile. He's moving his head about, trying to see.

"Fow mmone yeah?" He's got a toilet brush held aloft, his guitar strapped on backwards. I love this about Angus, he'll try anything.

"No sign of the killers yet, Angus."

"Ow." An old lady sees Malcolm and Mark tapping their swords in their palms. She grips her shopping trolley and walks back the way she came.

"What's with the gorilla suit, Angus?"

"Mumi oo ere," he says.

"What?" He drops the brush and removes the gorilla head, his hair sticking to the felt. He scratches his sweaty neck and snorts back a nostril full of snot.

"You're gunna wear a loin cloth and pull me onstage with a rope. I'll be in the cage on wheels, yeah. We pre-cut the bars so I can get out. You're gunna harass me and I'm gunna get all mad and chase you up onto the speakers, haw haw." His eyes light up, getting worked up already. "We set up a rope and you're gunna swing from one side of the stage to the other, out over the crowd." He's leaning into me with his furry arms and we watch the search party returning empty handed and I get to thinking this is the best job in the world and these guys are all mental.

"So you up to speed with the Tarzan act, Ron?" asks Ralph.

"Yeh, bloody good idea, except it's gunna be freezing cold."

"Oh, couple of bourbons, you won't feel a thing mate." I wasn't going to drink today, but with the pain in my mouth and the vibe of the show, a few bevies don't seem like such a bad idea. A rumble grows from up the street. Up drives a red American muscle car.

"Nice Corvette," says Phil, his eyes all glassy. He's always tonguing for fast cars, anything motorised, even remote control cars and boats. The Corvette is lipstick red, curved like lips too. He stops right beside us. The windows are tinted and we can't see the driver.

"Maybe that's your guy, Malcolm?" says Mark. The engine revs a small thunder. The body shakes.

"Give it to her," says Phil. The revs go high and thunderous and then the sound shifts to fast spinning. Smoke starts snaking off the back tyres, the wheels squeal. The back end swings 180 degrees, the engine louder still. We lose sight of the car in smoke, the chemical smell becoming taste. The wind blows and the red lipstick returns. Phil and Mark and Pat are yelling and screaming throwing fists in the air. The red blur speeds off. "Fuck yes," says Phil, "I'm getting one of those one day."

"Welcome to Geelong," says Ralph.

Angus and I spend the afternoon collecting palm leaves. Mark asks if he can dress up too, but Malcolm says no, only Angus and I. Ralph is running backwards and forwards between the mikes and sound desk repeating over and over, "CHECK, ONE, TWO, CHECK, CHECK, CHECK, ONE, TWO." Then he cranks up the reverb. "CHECK, CHECK, CHECK, CHECK, CHECK." Over the next few hours the fans start to arrive. I'm too amped to eat, instead a few bourbons and chatting with the fans, signing albums and t-shirts.

The hall can hold no more. The crowd is loud, waves of laughter rise and fall. Ralph plays his weird sound effect soundtrack. Police are everywhere but everyone's in line. The mayor tries to make a speech, but is booed off. There's girls on guys' shoulders and guys on girls' shoulders, kids sitting up in the window recesses. Malcolm and Mark and Phil go on to great applause and start playing *Baby Please Don't Go,* a rolling groovy beat.

Behind a curtain, Angus gets in the cage. He's so small he

can just about stand up. His guitar pokes out the bars. He says he's ready so I strip off and pick up the rope and start pulling. Pat holds the curtain back and the crowd goes quiet wondering what's going on. Then Angus starts jumping up and down shaking the bars and everyone starts whistling and killing themselves laughing. I sing the first and second verse with Angus playing his parts in the cage and me harassing him the whole time. I run from one side of the stage to the other feeling a little exposed in my loin cloth. I stop outside the cage and poke my tongue out and the gorilla breaks out and Angus jumps on me and we tussle for a bit, the people going ballistic, screaming and clapping.

I break loose and make my way to the side of the stage and Angus follows me so I jump up on the speakers. I grab an armful of rope and look down. Angus is jumping and I've never seen Malcolm happier. A wave of hesitation as I look out it's but too late. I grab an extra arms length and swing out and when I get to the middle I look back to the stage getting ready for my landing when I stop dead, hovering above the audience. I look down. A really tall bloke has grabbed the rope and is swinging it side to side, the band keep playing thinking this is hilarious. All the women make their way to the bottom of the rope, a pyramid of sorts building beneath me. I grip my legs tight trying to hold, maybe a thousand people in here all smiles.

The rope sways harder and my hands get sweaty, my arms getting tired, biceps hurting, my tongue pressing where my plate should be. I drop about a foot, still arms length above the crowd. There's a gasp and the band goes quieter, the gorilla watching too. My arms sting and I have to let go, falling into a cloud of screams and heads and hands. For a moment I float on their shoulders and then I drop, the ground hot and smelly and dark. My cloth is ripped off and hands pull all over. I try to stand up. Then Pat and Ralph charge in and grab me. Backstage I whip on some jeans, return to the stage and finish the set.

"What name is your reservation under, sir?" A middle aged bastard, with a strong posh accent peers at us over his glasses.

"Name? We're *AC/DC* for fucks sakes," I say. I've had a few too many, and I'm ready for bed.

"I'm sorry, sir," he says, "but we do not allow profanities in the lobby. Unless you can tell me what name the reservation is under, not some kind on moniker, then I cannot help you."

"Monkier?" says Angus, "I'm the bloody monkier." We all laugh. "Well, a gorilla, actually."

"Try the name Browning," says Malcolm. A few minutes later he gives us our keys.

"The girls are not on the reservation and will not be given admittance," he says. There's two girls with us, they ain't exactly small. We send them around the back and tell them to wait by the fire exit. Our room is on the third floor so we jump in the lift. Mark gets out on the first floor and goes to let them in. Someone's room smells like burning toast. The hallway has lights like streetlights on small steel frames. Inside I open the sliding door to the balcony and the sea breeze nearly pushes me back, sucking through the room and causing the doors to slam. "SSSHHHH," everyone gestures. Below there's a swimming pool glowing blue. Mark joins me on the balcony, hands me a bottle of whisky. I take a slug.

"Bet you ten bucks you wouldn't dive in from here." Was just thinking of jumping in anyway.

"Make it twenty."

"Deal," he says. I grab the bottle, take another swig, pull my jeans off, get up on the ledge and jump. Best not to think about these things. I aim for the end with the light, I guess it's the deep end. I dive head first, hands outstretched. Explosion entering the water. My hands smack in to the floor of the pool. I spring my legs off the floor and burst through the surface. "*Twenty bucks,*" I yell. I do a few laps and feel awake. A few people are having some drinks on their balcony. A couple of lights come on.

I get out and the breeze turns my skin to goose bumps, all the boys and the fat chicks have come out to watch me. "Let me in, you bastards," I yell. Phil disappears from the balcony, I assume to come let me in. The door to the pool area opens.

"Thanks, Phil," I'm rubbing my upper arms, but it's the Englishman from the front desk.

"What room number are you?" He rolls his r's.

"I dun know, came in a few minutes ago."

"The pool is open from 7a.m. to 7p.m. daily. I'm afraid that without a key, and no form of identification, I cannot grant you admittance at this time." His glasses, held together with a lanyard, rest on his upper chest.

"But I was just at the front desk, you spoke to me." A puddle is forming on the ground. Phil arrives.

"Bon you crazy mother—oh," he says.

"You got a key, Phil?" He dangles the leather circle between thumb and forefinger. I push past the clerk and fling up the stairs and wring my hair out on the hallway carpet. Phil hands me a joint and I take a few tokes. Head-spin. I walk through the main bedroom, in to the bathroom and grab a towel. One of the girls is on top of Mark in the bed.

I stand in front of the mirror. My shoulders hurt. The blind whips and snaps. I grab the string and open the fucking thing. As I do my stomach rumbles, my mouth fills with saliva. I run my hand through my hair. I swallow but it's no use. Hot all over. I run to the toilet. I feel how weak I am when I try to lift the lid. The bowl is full of piss but I don't have time to flush. Frothy spew, Coca-Cola black, mixes with the piss water.

I lie back against the cold tiles. I convulse and jerk my head over the bowl again. Bourbon taste works up through my sinuses and nostrils. Froth covers the surface of the water, slowly. A dark yellow line at the back of the bowl where the water drips. A hand rubs my back slowly. Another pulls my hair back. I don't fight. All my energy has gone.

"Here, honey, take a sip of this," says one of the girls. I take the glass but don't drink just yet. I rest my head back, close my eyes. She goes away and when she returns she wipes my face with a warm towel, runs the towel through my spewy hair.

"Come to bed," she says. Her big figure smothers me. I must look like a ragdoll with my bruised and battered head folded to one side. I feel her two hands beneath my armpits and to my surprise she lifts me easily, my sweaty back peeling, my feet dragging, my head hanging as she pulls me around the door ,back into the bedroom and lays me on the bed. She wraps me in blankets and keeps rubbing my back.

Soft and slow, she says, "You're okay now, darl." She's huge and half naked. Her boobs pale, her nipples the largest I've ever seen. Veins like trees, tiny and blue. Her belly, pressed against the bed, holds up her boob, her arms as big as my torso. Between the folds, silver sweat reflections. She has a likeable face. Her lipstick is smeared. Her eyelashes are really thin. Her big cow eyes open. She is a moving Mt Everest. I look around the room, everyone's asleep.

I can still taste spew in my mouth, the kind of heart burn feeling in your throat. Even with the blankets I'm still a little cold so I go to get in the sheets. I lift the top sheet and try to get in but my legs won't go in properly. Someone's short sheeted the bed, bastards.

She starts tying her hair up, struggling to reach her arms back. There's no mirror but she seems to be imagining herself. She starts talking about growing up in Perth and how her father is a wealthy miner and she and her mother fly to Melbourne for the weekend to go shopping. I don't tell her I grew up there but I ask her a few questions, which suburb she grew up in and where she went to school. At first she goes all quiet and then she answers.

I know she's lying and I tell her so, and then she starts crying, saying how she grew up on a farm in Tasmania, about her old man beating her up, about being a loner and running away from Devonport. About how no matter where she is she's always the same and her troubles follow her and she has to start all over again and so on and so forth.

Another spew wave comes, her perfume nearly tipping me over, my mouth filling with spit. I throw the blankets off and breath deep until the feeling goes. All the boys are snoring their heads off. My head is pounding.

"I'm sick of this," I say.

"I know, hon. It'll be over soon." I rest my elbows on my legs and my head in my hands. She keeps rubbing my back through the blanket.

"I mean this battle—sick and hungover over every morning, on the bus in the afternoon, drinking and gigging in the evening."

"Don't worry about that now."

"That's all I can think about."

"You want my opinion?" she says. "What I saw last night, the experience I had, the looks on everyone's faces; happy and fascinated. You got the school boy, what's his name?'

"Angus."

"He's good to watch, but you're the one. You give the music feeling, and flavour, like a good wine."

"Don't talk about wine right now," I heave.

"Dear little soul. You know what I mean. Seems to me if you can lay off the booze and focus on the music, you'll be fine hon. Nothing's a fairy story." She's rubbing my hair back.

"Why are you so nice?"

"Look at me, Bon. I don't have a choice."

'I don't even know what your name is." The blind slaps on the window frame.

"Rosie," she says. "Can you do something for me? Write a song about me? I don't care if you're mean or nasty or nice. I don't care if you talk about how fat I am, I just want to be noticed for once. Can you do that?"

"Sure, why not? But I gotta admit, I just steal ideas from old blues songs. The older the better, cause no one recognises them. I'm trying to write my own songs, but it's not that easy. Everyone thinks the lyrics are a piece of piss and I can just bang out a hundred songs a day."

DEAR SUZY,

SORRY TO HAVE MISSED YOU IN MELBOURNE, BUT WE COULDN'T WAIT TO GET OUT OF ~~HERE~~ THERE. I'VE BEEN IN EVERYONE'S BAD BOOKS LATELY SO I'M HAPPY TO BE IN SYDNEY, RECORDING ~~SONGS~~ AT ALBERTS. GOOD NEWS IS THAT WE'RE OFF TO EUROPE IN A FEW WEEKS AND GOOD TIMING CAUSE THIS COUNTRY IS DOING MY HEAD IN. HIGH VOLTAGE MADE GOLD ALBUM LAST WEEK AND I SENT MY COPY TO MUM TO PUT ON HER MANTLEPIECE. SHE TOLD ME TO CLEAN THE SONG LYRICS UP, BUT THAT AIN'T GUNNA HAPPEN. LONG WAY TO THE TOP IS BEING RELEASED IN ENGLAND THE DAY WE FLY OUT, BUT THE BAND IS COMPLETELY DIFFERENT NOW. I'LL SEND YOU OUR ADDRESS IN LONDON AS SOON AS I KNOW.

TAKE CARE TWEETY,
RON.

We cross Botany Bay's swamps to Sydney airport. We hardly speak. Mark's happy to be leaving because the husband of the bird he's been fucking has started to ask about him at the hotel. We check in our bags and after a lot of arguing they let Angus take his guitar on the plane. On the other side of security is the *Countdown* camera crew, with Ian Meldrum in his stupid hat. He waddles up and shakes everyone's hands.

"Hello, Ian," I say. "Punched any girls out lately?" He frowns, his cheeks drooping, and shakes my question off. We sit together with our backs to the runway. One of the crew holds a microphone over our heads with a long stick.

"First of all," he says, "it's just gone like that, BANG, into the charts." This cracks me up, I throw my head back in disbelief, he hasn't been paying attention, as usual. I wipe my sweaty hand on my jeans. "What do you think you owe your success to?"

"Ahhh..." says Angus.

"It's *nothing* to do with us at all," I say, waving my hand, trying to collect my thoughts. "Our success is due to the taste of the public." This stumps Ian.

"Well, you've just lost me for words," he says, frowning.

"But it was a hard climb for a while wasn't it?"

"Yeah," I say, "we worked for eighty bucks a night for a while, but Angus rolls his shorts up, you know." Ian turns to Malcolm and Angus.

"How long has Bon been in the band?"

"Twelve months," says Malcolm.

"Twelve months," repeats Ian, surprised. "Bon has been playing in Australia for a long time now, going back ten years to the Valentines, where did you find him?" I put my best old man voice on.

"I was living in Adelaide, getting very old and grey, and this bloke called D—what's his name?"

"Dennis," says Phil.

"Yes, Dennis Laughlin, an old friend of mine who's the manager of the band."

"*Was,*" says Phil.

"He says, ah, *Want a job with a rock and roll band?* and I went; *I don't know if I can do that mate, they're all pretty young looking fellas, ya know, cause I'm a bit of a grand daddy.*" Hard to tell if Ian's listening or not, so I address him. "Don't tell anyone, Ian, but I was a bit sneaky. They were a pretty cheesy band. I could see what they were trying to do and where I could take them. Anyway, we went around to Bruce's basement in Prospect Road and had a blow. It was incredible. A couple of days later I went to have a medical for a job at the fertiliser factory." I'm lying. It was for a ship painter in Adelaide harbour, but you don't want these writers knowing the whole truth. "And I thought fuck that. So I rang Dennis and said send me sixty bucks for the next plane. Two days later I'm singing *Can I Sit Next to You Girl."*

"How old are you now?" asks Ian, sitting on the edge of his seat.

"I'm twenty eight now. These blokes are nineteen and twenty, and I'm gunna have to keep up with them, so I bought a stack of methedrine. I drag them here and there, usually down." Everyone laughs. The pilots walk by, watching.

"Yeah," says Angus, ashing his cigarette, "especially when he's up and down like a human kangaroo."

"With the success that your music has had in Australia," says Ian, "are you going over there thinking you can take on the English market?" I look over at Malcolm. He looks so bored, he cracks me up. Either than or he's hungover as hell.

"Yeah," he says, "we're confident. We're not over confident, but we're very confident."

***

The area around our gate has six lines of chairs, all running parallel. There's eight of us and we have to sit separately. "You think our plane will crash?" asks Angus.

"Probably, and everyone except you will live," says Malcolm. Angus starts picking his nose and wiping the boogies under the seats. His finger gets right in there.

"Pick a winner, Angus?" asks Phil.

"Slippery bugger keeps going deeper." The holding area fills up. On the loud speaker we receive notification that the plane will be delayed due to catering complications. Opposite us, a grey haired guy in a tan trench coat stands up and paces back and forwards a few times. He scratches his head. The gates open and we all start lining up. The guy in the trench coat pushes in front of Angus. Angus pushes him back. The guy doesn't move much and he's about two foot taller than Angus. He moves back in when Pat, Ralph, Mark, Phil, Malcolm, Browning and I surround him.

"Alright. Alright," he says, and walks away.

Angus takes the window seat, with a spare between us, so he can play his guitar. Brand new strings all shiny. He's nervous. He opens and closes the window shutter, reads the magazine, plays his guitar, reads the menu, fiddles with the seatbelt. He pops his pimples. "Goodbye, Steak and Kidney," he says.

The stewardesses runs through the safety procedures. The engines go from a dull rumble to a loud roar. Bumps in the runway, house roofs and trees blur, the flaps in the wings move up and down, the landing gear thuds back. As the plane tilts, I see the harbour and the opera house. My ears pop. Angus clutches the arm rest, his nose twitching like a rabbit. I lay my chair back and pull one of the sleeping masks on.

Me and Suzy in our flat on Canning Highway. I was working at the bakery and going to church to become a Catholic so we could get married and have kids. Petra Street, East Fremantle. Brian's parents' place. Beatles posters on the wall. There was a single bed with stuffed toys. Sharon Smythe and her bangles. We pecked. I kissed her neck and licked her ears. I pulled off her knickers. Voices were outside. She pushed me back and took my belt off, pulling my jeans half off. I sucked her breasts. She opened her legs and I slipped in. She thrust in and sent me over but I had to withdraw as she wasn't on the pill. She grabbed my shirt but cum got on a teddy.

Suzy looked at me. Mad. I had to apologise for weeks.

A tapping on my shoulder.

"Today's menu is chicken parmigiana or roast beef," the stewardess says, pushing the brake on the cart.

"Got any spag bol?" asks Angus.

"I'm sorry sir, I think they serve spaghetti on the Bahrain leg."

"I thought they'd serve it on a... plate," he chuckles. "I'll have the chicken pyjamas then." The new Superman movie trailer is being projected on the screen. I order a few whiskeys. Clark Kent flies around the world, throws glaciers onto infernos, saves millions of people, rids the world of evil, but cannot fall in love. Lois is oblivious. Two speeding trains going full speed at one another only have to miss by an inch. He flies home via the moon. I take my compendium out of the net and jot a few lines.

EVERYBODY FLOATING ACROSS THE AIR
BIGMAN NOWHERE AROUND
COME HERE SWEETHEART CHANGE YOUR ATTITUDE
CAUSE IT'S A LOW WAIT NOW
WE'RE ALL SEARCHING FOR A FREE RIDE
THINKING ABOUT A GRAVY TRAIN
IT'S A TURN, IT'S THE SAME, IT'S - A PETRIFIED
AND ~~NO ONE~~ EVERYONE'S TO BLAME

Angus goes to the toilet and when he returns he puts his arms out rising and falling over people's heads and makes his body into the shape of a plane. A *DDDDDRRRRRR* exits his mouth. The seat belt lights come on and he's asked to sit and the pilot says we're about to hit some turbulence. He straps his seatbelt on and grabs the arm rests. His energy levels go to another level. I'm pretty drunk by now because Angus doesn't drink and we order for the two of us. The no smoking light comes on. I look across and Malcolm and Mark are dead to the world. Phil is staring out the window.

The pen I'm using bursts and massive blotches of ink spread in my notebook. Angus grabs the pen and starts flicking ink all over the place. The mood on the plane is taking a dive, they dim the lights, but then to make it worse the big fat guy in front of us spews straight into his window, chunks spattered all up the walls. The stench fills the cabin, making me feel sick too.

"Bon," Angus says, "how long til you reckon we play at

Albert Hall?"

"Next week I think, Angus."

I'm almost out of whisky, the stewardesses are strapped in near the kitchen. Out the window I see clouds. Vooomp. The plane drops a couple of hundred feet and Angus the sicko is daring me to kiss the granny near us as he reckons she'll be up for some smooching as we're going to crash. So I look over and she's looking back and I throw her a peck in the air and she doesn't even flinch, she's pecking right back. She cups her boob as well and I'm put in my place and Angus is cracking up, showing his rotting teeth. If there was a white one in there it'd be a snooker set.

After what feels like a week, we land at Heathrow, greeted by Browning himself. I need a shower. Outside, there's a limousine waiting, long and black, like English clouds. We sip champagne and memories of Fraternity come flooding back. All this means so much to me, I go quiet. The limo does the tour of all the big sights, the boys letting go, showing excitement and emotion. We drive over the river near the Tower and Browning thinks it's a good time to tell us that our first tour has been canceled, for now. *Back Street Crawler* can't do it. Kossoff overdosed a couple of days ago.

GONE SHOOTIN'
LONDON -- 1976

DEAR SUZY,

BEEN TWIDDLING OUR THUMBS FOR A FEW WEEKS BECAUSE OUR TOUR WITH BACK STREET CRAWLER WAS CANCELED AFTER AN INCIDENT WITH THEIR LEAD SINGER. WE'RE LIVING IN THIS MASSIVE TERRACE HOUSE IN BAYSWATER WHICH IS CLOSE TO THE CITY SO WE'VE BEEN CHECKING OUT THE MUSEUMS AND ART GALLERIES AND THE LIKE.

GOOD TO BE BACK IN LONDON EXCEPT FOR THIS ONE TIME WHEN I WENT BACK TO THE HOTEL BRUCE AND I WORKED AT TO SEE IF ANYONE STILL WORKED THERE AND NEXT THING I KNOW I'VE BEEN WALLOPED ON THE HEAD WITH A GLASS JUG. SURGERY TO RESET MY JAW AND A WEEKS REST TO LET THE BRUISING GO DOWN. BONUS WAS THE MONEY I DIDN'T SPEND WHILE IN HOSPITAL I PUT TOWARD A TAILORED SET OF WHITE LEATHER TAILS. ALSO THE DENTIST'S FINALLY FIXED MY BROKEN PLATE.

WE'RE PLAYING OUR FIRST SHOW TOMORROW NIGHT IN HAMMERSMITH AND THEN OFF TO EUROPE TO TOUR WITH RITCHIE BLACKMORE'S 'RAINBOW.' IF THE EUROPEAN SHOWS GO WELL, WE'RE OFF TO AMERICA AND MIGHT MAKE SOME MONEY AT LONG LAST...

TAKE CARE

BON

HI IRENE,

SORRY I HAVEN'T WRITTEN IN A WHILE, I'VE BEEN TOO STONED. THERE'S ENOUGH HASH IN LONDON TO KEEP ADELAIDE SUPPLIED FOR ABOUT A DECADE. A REAL BONUS IS ATLANTIC LET US TAKE WHATEVER RECORDS WE WANT FROM THEIR VAULTS SO I GO THERE ABOUT TWICE A WEEK AND LISTEN TO WHATEVER TICKLES MY FANCY.

I HEARD YOU WERE PREGNANT. ALTHOUGH IT BREAKS MY HEART TO HEAR IT, I HOPE YOU'RE HAPPY. CONGRATS. DID YOU HEAR VINCE HAD A BABY? THE CUNT. BET HE WASHES ALL THE NAPPIES.

I SHOULD BE HOME FOR CHRISTMAS AND BACK IN SYDNEY IN JAN FOR MORE RECORDING. WE'RE WORKING FLAT OUT HERE AND NEXT WEEK WE'LL BE THE BIGGEST BAND IN THE WORD. I MIGHT EVEN BE ABLE TO PAY YOU BACK THE FIFTY BUCKS I OWE YA. AIN'T NO FUN WAITIN' ROUND TO BE A MILLIONAIRE.

LOVE YA, BON.

While Ralph and Pat load up the Transit van, the rest of us catch the tube to Hammersmith. We're playing at The Red Cow, a fairly unknown joint Browning has booked at the last minute because the tour has fallen through the arse. The place is tiny, a dinky little joint that if you jump you can touch the ceiling, even us short arses. Inside there's ornate ceiling roses and wooden architraves. Near the front door is a small bar that serves one type of beer and ten different spirits. The stage, if you can call it that, is five yards across. Out back, the band room is nearly bigger than the front room. I don't care, we haven't played in weeks so we're all bursting out of our skins.

There's about ten people sitting at the bar, and half of those look like they live here. We start playing and they all laugh at us, at Angus. He provokes them and runs riot. We're so loud it feels like the building is about to collapse. We play better than ever. Everything clicks. We go full on like there's a thousand people here. Our first show in London. After our first set I walk straight off the stage to the bar. People start leaving. Maybe I'm cursed. Maybe England has it in for me. I order a few whiskeys and start to wipe myself out.

As we start our second set, people start pouring in the door, they come in groups of five or more. By the time we play *Problem Child,* our angular off-beat delinquent song, the place is full. The people at the front are forced closer and closer to us. To my surprise one of them is Margaret, my stunning root rat from Adelaide. When the lights flash I catch a good look at her, smiling and rocking, her hand bag swinging. I gesture for her to meet me out back.

After the show I feel high, real high, like I haven't in a long time. I'm buzzing and shaking when I pick up my glass. I sit but stand again, my temperature running high. Angus and Malcolm go straight home. Mark's at the bar. Phil helps Pat and Ralph with the van. I'm pacing up and back.

"Brothel creepers, comfy fuckin shoes aye?" I know the voice. When I turn around there's a stocky bloke with long brown hair and dark eyebrows. Eyes like a wolf. Ozzy-fuckin-Osbourne. "Got a few pairs myself," he says, giving me a hug. "Would you take a look at this guy, Thelma?" Thelma and I shake hands, she flicks her massive fringe out the way.

"Fuckin brilliant mate, jus-fuckin brilliant," says Ozzy. "You guys." He burps, but holds it in. "You guys are gunna, be, massive. You got it. I'm callin' our manager tomorrow, you cunts are touring with us. If they don't bring yous with us, I'm quittin', I don't give a fuck."

"Ozzy!" says Thelma, giving him a *take it easy* look.

"Fuck 'em," he says, "Tommi could take a few chapters out of Angus' book." He's waving his hand with a fag between his stained fingers. "What's the name of the song with the full on ending? The one 'bout the child?"

"*Problem Child*," I say.

"Un-fuckin-believeable. Thought my teeth were gunna rattle out me head. The pauses, fuck. Wish we wrote that." He moves his free hand through his hair. "How long you here for?"

"A while," I say, sweat making my back itchy. "We had some shows lined up with *Back Street Crawler*, but now it looks like we're gunna tour with Ritchie Blackmore."

"Fuckin *Deep Purple*," he says. "You boys won't get along, I can tell yas now. Right. Where's your manager? We'll get him and our manager together, work something out." I see Margaret standing in the door. My heart jumps. She's wearing a blue velvet outfit, her long black hair draped over her front.

"Good to see ya anyway, Bon, you know last time I saw you, after that Myponga show? The one in the middle of fuckin' nowhere?"

"Yeah," I say, "in South Australia."

"We stopped in Perth on the way back, to refuel and shit. I stood on the fuckin' runway and had a fag. Took my shirt off, it was so fuckin' hot. Swear I was gunna melt. I think I'm still sunburnt." He lifts up his shirt and shows us his tits. "Been about two years, fuck me." We have a good laugh. Margaret moves in and we hug, the velvet on my skin, the earthy smell of her hair. A bolt of energy in my body, a sting in my heart.

"Ozzy and Thelma, this is my friend from Adelaide, Margaret," I say.

"*Silver*," she says, "call me Silver. I had no idea you were playing, Bon. I've never been in here before, and here you are." Her voice rises and falls and she has an energy that's infectious. "My friend Martin rang me in the break and told me to get here. I can't believe it's you. So good to see you." Ozzy and Thelma shoot off, Ozzy repeating that he'll be in touch. Silver and I sit down and stare into each other's eyes, holding hands.

"What's with the name change?" I ask her.

"Oh, I've been Silver for a few years now. I've been traveling the States, no one calls me Margaret anymore."

"You're not married anymore?" She takes out a small silver case and offers me a cigarette. I refuse.

"No. No. No," she says. "That ended as well." This guy comes up to us. He's wearing a blue jacket that's had the colour stripped by rain. His jeans are torn. He's skinny and pale. He grabs a chair and sits close to us, looking at me intensely. He checks his watch and his shoes smell like mould.

"Hallo," he says. "Name's Leroy. Leroy Kincaid."

"How are ya, mate?" I ask him.

"Olrite, olrite, can't complain," he says, his voice is like a giant's voice trapped inside a tiny body. "Nice show," he says. "Good set you got going." He flings his head, looks around the room.

"You enjoy that, did ya?" I ask.

"Oh, specially the little man, what's his name?"

"Angus."

"Fucking mental fuck, isn't he? You lot from Australia then?"

"Yeah mate, from the land of Oz." Silver gives me a raised eyebrow look.

"Oh ay, naw, I meant the band, from Australia?"

"Yep."

"What's it like there? Tonnes o' unemployment, crime, corruption?" A bubble of spit shoots out his mouth.

"Guess so mate, everything's a bit strange." Silver lights a cigarette, her red lips wet.

"We have to get going soon, Bon," she says, as if we had

somewhere to go.

"You got all these scallys hanging round the streets," says Leroy, looking at me intense, "beating up old ladies, breaking into houses. There's nowhere to live, no jobs, nothing to do. The government are telling us to leave. What I want to know is, what you doing about it? You got other bands out there, The Sex Pistols, The Clash, making a statement." I look at Silver and sip my bourbon.

"What do you suppose we should do then, Mister?" I ask him.

"You should get all your fans, right, when you've got 'em in the palm of your hand, to join us and storm Westminster. Once we're inside, we'll stay there until they give the people their land back, if they refuse we'll burn the place down."

"What about everyone inside?" asks Silver, frowning, holding her cigarette away from her face.

"Fuck 'em," he says. "They got nothin to live for. There's a hung parliament no matter which way. Might as well start again. *Who governs Britain?* No one fuckin' governs Britain, that's who. What a bunch of twats. They want anarchy, we'll give em anarchy."

"It'll never happen," says Silver, her legs folded tight.

"Why not?" asks Leroy, getting agitated.

"Everyone's too stoned," I say.

"Because the army and police will step in, that's why," says Silver. "Don't you read the newspapers?"

"Oh fuck off," he says, standing up, pointing at us. "I'm warning ya, when the walls go up in flames, you better know which side you're on." He walks off and starts chatting to someone near the door. They look over and point. I look back.

Silver and I take a cab to her place in Kensington. Her pad is at the top of four flights of stairs, a converted attic. The ceiling rises to a peak in the middle, where a single lightbulb hangs. She had some Aussie artist paint the walls like the night sky.

There's the Southern Cross and Orion's belt which makes the room feel much bigger than it is. Her bed is retracted against the wall. A small lamp and a bedside table with books piled high. An oval mirror sits above a small desk with her trinkets and boxes full of jewelery and make up. Silver comes out with a tray of tea and some ginger nut biscuits. She's chatting away the whole time about how her marriage broke up, how she finally left her horrible family, how she flew from Adelaide to Sydney then to Los Angeles. How she worked her way across America meeting heaps of people and having the time of her life. She's a good story teller and makes me feel welcome. She's the most beautiful woman I've ever met. Her soft skin has a gold glow that stands out against her dark hair. Her face is so perfect, all the bits are in the right place. I want to kiss her. Under the window, a chrome trunk full of records. She finishes her story and apologises for not flipping the record, for talking too much. When she asks me a question I get half-way through my first sentence and she goes off on another tangent. I take my boots off and put my feet up on the coffee table.

"Comfortable there?" she asks. Resting her head on the base of her palm.

"I like to put my feet up, and other parts of my body," I say.

"Oh, God," she says, amused. "You carry on like you work hard or something."

"I do. All the touring takes it out of you."

"Yeah, right," she says.

"How do you afford all this then?" I ask.

"I'm working my butt off that's how, and it's none of your business, mister," she chuckles. "Bet I've traveled more than you have."

"Wanna bet?" I say. From the bureau she takes out a wooden box and then brings out a bag of powder. Her hair is tied back besides a strand she lets fall in her face. She keeps chatting, saying nothing about the drugs. I recall Browning in the hospital, after I overdosed, telling me to stay off the shit. Her hands work fast, tapping, cutting, taking occasional drags on her cigarette. She snorts a line and throws her head back. Her pupils dilate, her eyes are nearly the colour of her hair.

"You want one?" she asks. I'm sitting with my arms crossed.

"No, I'm not allowed."

"What do you mean, *you're not allowed*?"

"The band would fire me if they found out."

"Wow, man, what kind of regime you got yourself into?"

"Got any whisky?" I ask.

"Have a look," she says, pointing to the kitchen. "There might be some left after our last party. I don't usually drink." I go into the kitchen and open the cupboards. No booze. I step back and look up. A bottle of gin. Good enough. I think of that guy, Leroy, from the Red Cow. Should we be more serious? More political? I squeeze some lemon juice into the glass and when I return Silver's still chatting away though I've lost what she's talking about. I see the razor on the table. The powder ready to go. She goes into the bathroom and I flip the record over and scribble a few lines.

I GOT MY ~~ADDICTIONS~~ FAVOURITE VICES,
I GOT MY FAVOURITE DRUGS
BUT WASN'T TIL I SAW YOU ~~AGAIN~~
TONIGHT, THAT I FELL IN LOVE.
DIDN'T KNOW WHAT I WAS MISSING,
CARRYING AROUND THIS HOLE,
DON'T ~~WANT~~ NEED TO WIPE MYSELF OUT,
NO MORE LOSING CONTROL.

~~I SEE YOU COMING~~ WHEN YOU COME MY WAY,
IT'S A FEELING THAT A MAN CAN'T BLUFF.
I'M ADDICTED TO YOU, I'M ADDICTED TO
YOU, I FELL IN LOVE WITH YOU.
SHE ~~TAKES~~ STEALS ALL MY CIGARETTES,
SHE STEALS ALL MY BOOZE
SHE SELLS ALL MY FURNITURE, FORCES ME TO CHOOSE.

~~THEY~~ YOU TELL ME SHE'S ALL BAD, TAKE ME FOR A RIDE

SMASH MY HEAD WITH A LOAF OF
BREAD, TIL I WAKE UP INSIDE.
OH WOMAN YOU RUN ME ROUND, ALL OVER TOWN
BUT LISTEN HERE, I DON'T CARE,
EVERYONE KNOWS I'M A ~~CLOWN~~????

***

One step, two steps, three steps into the bus. My hand slides along the silver rail that curves up and leads into the dark cavern. Phil's in the driver's seat, finishing a can of Coke. His seat is black leather. All the others are brown corduroy. I take my place a few rows back, traffic noise becomes a murmur. Grey cloud and thin trees, the drizzle that is Germany. I like to spot the homes, like little shacks, smoke rising from the chimneys. This is the last part of our tour of England, Scotland, and Western Europe. All cold food, fast women and warm beer.

At the venue we're shown our room and get ready. There's a long black bench beneath a long mirror surrounded by white bulbs. Malc is flicking through a copy of *Rolling Stone*. Angus is restringing his guitar. A guy walks in wearing khaki pants, a white polo shirt with pens in the front pocket. His name tag says 'Gerard — Promotion Coordinator'. He has a round face. Attached to his belt is a walkie talkie that keeps buzzing.

"Okay, everybody," he says, holding a clip board. "Ritchie is delighted to have you on this tour, but there are a few things he has asked you to do and not do, before, during and after the show." Phil, testing his drum sticks on the ground, looks up at me. Malc gets up and goes to the toilet. Angus is tuning up. Mark is elsewhere. "Guys?" he says in his German accent. "Okay, number one, have lots of fun. Two, no liquids, fire, ash or chemicals to be spilt or thrown on stage. Three, do not enter Ritchie's dressing room under any circumstances." Malc comes back, lights up a smoke, looks into the mirror and checks his teeth.

"What's your name, mate?" I ask.

"Gerard. Now, as I was saying. Four, no one to come backstage until after Rainbow have finished."

"Excuse me, Gerard," I say, "I have a question."

"Ya."

"Yeah, um, mate," I say, "can I bring my mum backstage? She's flown over from Australia just for the show. She loves Ritchie and the Rainbow."

"Of course your mother can come backstage."

"Five, no—"

"Can my mum come backstage too?" asks Angus.

"Ya. Just if we—"

"What about your mum, Phil?"

"Yeah, what about my mum, Gerard?" asks Phil.

"All your mothers can come. As I was saying, rule number five, make no reference to the Rainbow during your show." Malc, furious, starts reading from the *Rolling Stone* he's holding.

"Listen to this," he says. "*Those concerned with the future of hard rock may take solace in knowing that with the release of the first U.S. Album by these Australian gross-out-champions, the genre has unques...*" he stutters, "*unquestionably hit its all time low. Lead singer Bon Scott spits out his vocals with a truly annoying aggression which, I suppose, is the only way to do when all you seem to care about is being a star so that you can get laid every night. Stupidity bothers me. Calculated stupidity offends me.*" He throws the magazine at the mirror.

Angus' unplugged guitar stops twanging. Gerard gives up on his list, and says, "I will return when you have five minutes left," and leaves.

"Fuck 'em," says Phil, his voice deep.

"They're lying," I say. "I hardly ever get laid, I have to pull myself most of the time. Don't I? *Don't I, Phil?*"

"Yes, Bon," says Phil.

"There goes our chances of an American tour," says Malc. "Where's Browning? Why isn't Browning talking to these pricks?" The door swings open and in walks Mark, all excited.

"Oh my God, you guys you better come quick, you won't believe this shit, quick, quick, quick, quick, quick." He's waving like he's stirring a bowl of pancake mixture. I tell him I'm not in the mood, but he grabs my arm. Phil and I follow him along the corridors. We come to a door with a handmade 'Ritchie Blackmore' sign sticky taped on. Mark puts his ear to the door, looks up and back along the corridor.

"You not gunna believe this shit," he says. "I haven't seen anything like this since Toowoomba."

"Okay, Mark, open the door," says Phil.

"Quick, quick, quick," says Mark. Inside there are about two hundred lit candles, mostly matchstick, but some fat coffee tin ones. Strong honey smell.

"How's about this bloke, eh?" says Mark.

"What a wally-woofter," says Phil. In amongst some champagne, I spot a bottle of whisky and tuck it in my denim jacket. Mark and Phil start blowing the candles out. I start blowing too, the room filling up with smoke, gradually getting darker and darker. Mark starts laughing between blows, and I start laughing and Phil too.

"Leave a couple lit so we can find our way outta here," says Mark, having a chuckle. After a while you learn that you can't control everything. Before that, you only have the feeling that you can't control everything. Phil opens the door, filling the room with hallway light and Mark grabs two six packs of beer.

"Let's hit the frog and toad, fellas," whispers Phil.

"What'd you do?" asks Malcolm.

"Ritchie's room was full of candles," says Mark, "so we blew them all out."

"They're gunna know it's us," says Malcolm, who's changed into his black 'show' t-shirt.

"Who gives a fuck," says Mark. Malcolm doesn't answer but gives Mark an intense look. There's a knock at the door. We all act casual, I pick up the *Rolling Stone*. In walks Browning, our manager. He has one of the tour laminates around his neck.

"I have some bad news," he says. "There's been an accident." He interlaces his fingers. "Ralph was up in a crane rigging up the lighting and he was electrocuted. He was thrown out of the cage and fell to the floor."

"Jesus Christ," I say.

"The ambulance came and took him to the hospital," says Browning. "They said he'll be okay, a few broken ribs and internal bruising. I've arranged for a replacement for the remainder of the tour and I'll look for a more permanent replacement for when we return to London."

"Who made you the boss?" asks Malcolm.

"Can we go see him in the hospital?" asks Phil. Browning ignores Malcolm and says we might be able to go to the hospital in the morning but there's a tight turn around as we have to be in Dusseldorf early tomorrow. Malcolm runs his hand through his hair and lifts his guitar up and slides the strap over his shoulders. Angus keeps quiet. He knows when Malcolm is in a bad mood. In walks Gerard, a lighter in his hand.

"Very funny joke with the candles," he says, "but please don't make my job more hard." Malcolm takes a scull of his beer, and then speaks very quietly, but with great fury in his eyes.

"Get the fuck out. We're preparing for the show, now fuck off." Gerard looks like he's about to cry. I want to hug him.

"Take it easy, Malcolm," says Browning.

"You stay out of it," Malcolm says to Browning. "Where are our American visas?"

"Malcolm, calm down," says Browning, unafraid, looking all of us in the eyes. "You know I'm working on it. We've spoken about this already."

We go on stage and play as hard as possible.

The sun is out and so are our hangovers. We run out of time

to see Ralph in the hospital so I grab a plastic bag and yellow envelope from hotel reception and duck into the toilets. I never remember which is which, 'herren' or 'damen', man or woman? I lay the bag on the floor, luckily it's a dry log. Must be from the schnitzels and chips. I finish the second half on the proper toilet. I wrap the log several times and spray it with air freshener. I drop the bag inside the yellow envelope. I ask the concierge for a pen and write.

DEAR RALPH (BEST SPIDER IN THE WORLD),

SORRY TO HEAR EVERYTHING HAS TURNED TO SHIT. HOPE YOU GET BETTER SOON.
SEE YOU BACK IN AUSTRALIA MATE.

BON.

Along the edge I write in big bold letters FRAGILE and the address. We take our usual spots and the bus bumps out. A mixture of old and new buildings and always the vibe of the Soviets across the border. Phil finds an English radio station and we get as far as the first set of traffic lights. Mark yells out that he's forgotten his jacket. So we pull over and Mark runs back to the hotel. Phil and I share a joint as he prepares to enter driving mode. We catch the tail end of a news break. *The forty two year old man's body was found in the bathroom of his Memphis home.* As soon as I hear Memphis I know it's Elvis. Malc and Angus and Browning crowd around the front. I grab my asthma puffer and take a few hits.

"Fuckin' hell," says Angus.

"You seen any recent photos of him?" asks Phil. "He looked totally different."

"Another one bites the dust," says Browning, hanging from the overhead rail like a monkey. Mark returns short of breath, his jacket in his fist. We descend the on-ramp of the autobahn, the leafless trees beginning to blur. I stay up front and listen to the obituary and they play *Blue Suede Shoes* and *Love Me Tender* and *Heartbreak Hotel* and I don't even sing along. Cars speed past in the inside lane and the skies are low and overcast. I feel like I've lost a friend. I get the urge to write a letter to Suzy and Irene and Silver. I take my bag down from the overhead compartment and rifle though, looking for my notebook. No luck. I look through the whole bus.

"Looking for something?" asks Malcolm.

"Yeah, com-pen..." I scratch my arm. "My black book. You seen it?"

"Nah."

"Shit," I say. I ask everyone else, but no dice.

"We have to go back," I say.

"No chance. We can't go back now," says Malcolm, shaking his head. "We have interviews."

"*I* have interviews," I say.

"We're late already, Bon. Got any lyrics in it?"

"A few ideas, yeah, and some letters and things."

"We'll ring the hotel when we get to Ludwig-watchya-call-it."

"Oh for fuck's sakes," I say. "You went back for Mark's jacket."

"We'll ring 'em at the next town," says Malcolm. Fuck it. I sit up the front and roll a joint for Phil and I. A black cloud falls over the bus and with it a spell of homesickness for old Ronald Belford Scott, longing for the sun and the windy fresh air of Fremantle. Dad and Dereck and Graeme all eating snags and bread in the jarrah grandstand watching the football. Mum buying fruit and veg at the markets, everyone walking around barefoot. *Maybe all of my bands are doomed to fail, oh yes.*

"Hey Bon mate," says Phil. In his blood shot eyes is a calmness. He drives to be switched off. "I got an idea for a T.V. show." He steers with one hand at the centre of the wheel.

"Oh yeah, Phil, what's it called?"

"*I'm a Real Cunt Job,*" he says. "It's about this bloke named Ron, he's a real cunt. All he wants to do is to settle down with a wife and kids, and a dog and chickens. But somehow he always ends up travelling, never settling anywhere." Phil sucks on a straw in a Coke can and his cheeks close in.

"Sounds like a real cunt," I say. "I can see him alright, I bet he has brown wavy hair, tattoos, and a missing tooth."

"Yeah that's him, you got him, will you—"

"I bet everyone thinks women just throw themselves at him willy nilly."

"Yeh, closer..."

"I bet he thinks he can drink like a camel but in reality he can only handle two beers and then after that he picks fights with everyone."

"You got it," says Phil.

"I bet the cunt never has any money, cause he always loses it or gives it away, ya know."

"Yeah that's him alright."

"What a cunt."

"So, what do you reckon, good idea for a show?"

"Who the bloody hell would watch *that*?" I ask.

"Maybe you're right," says Phil. "But I've been thinking, maybe I'll go back to New Zealand and open a restaurant. Stay in one place for a while."

***

We drive the bus onto the overnight ferry and arrive in foggy London as the sun is rising. Dead leaves float and swirl. Phil parks and we all start gathering our stuff and I can't wait to get to Silver's place. Browning stands up the front of the bus and says there's going to be a band meeting tomorrow and we all have to be there. We get inside and I have a shower and a shave. I take out my dental plate and give it a wash and begin to feel short of breath, a few shots from my puffer. The basin full of hot water, I lather some soap, wipe it along my jaw and bring the razor to my skin. My eyes are all puffed. I need a hair cut. I feel like a ten year old pair of shoes that haven't had a retread. The pendant Silver gave me dangles from the chain on my neck. My eyebrows need a prune. These stupid tattoos? A lion? A parrot? A snake with a sword? What was I thinking?

I move the razor through the soap. A path clears on my bumpy broken jaw skin. Wash the razor, tap the hair out. *The meeting. Fuck me. This is it. It's over.* I try to utter the words *same as every other band,* but I can't speak. *Have they found another singer?* I run some more hot water. I pull my cheek skin up and shave along my jaw. *No visas. My drug conviction, surely.* I wipe my face with the towel, put my plate back in and a smile in the mirror. *The drinking?* Malcolm and Mark drink as much as me. I look myself in the eye. I wince. I chuck my shaving kit in my room and head for Silver's.

London, the greatest city in the world, if you allow it. On The Tube I grow more and more excited to see her. I make up names for the stations: Rabbit Warren Street, Who-ston, Kings Angry, Saint Pancreas. When we are apart she takes up all my thoughts. Only when the band plays do I forget her. I buy roses and a small trinket box made of wood and silver. My boots clang heavily on the four flights of wooden stairs that go up to Silver's attic, she opens the door and she's more beautiful than I remember. My sphincter clenches in excitement. "Oh, Bon," she says, unamused with the flowers. She wears black jeans, a black leather jacket and her hair is braided. Her waist is white and pure, soft. I tell her about the tour and we drink tea and listen to music and make love. The Southern Cross painting is lit up by moonlight. We talk about Elvis dying and then fall asleep. *There's a glass plate over his coffin. Inside he's awake, and he's talking. I'm the only one who can see he's alive.*

My right shoulder rises and falls, getting nudged. "Close the window," Silver says. "The mozzies are getting in." I pull a pillow over my face to drown out the light, the outside noise. She gets up, naked, and closes the window and jumps back in, her hands freezing cold on my back. I squirm. She turns the lamp on, lights a cigarette and starts reading. "Listen to this, Bon," she says, reading from one of her books. The bed jolts every time she jumps to catch a mozzie.

Silver puts on her school teacher voice, "*I was thinking of very old times, when the Romans first came here, nineteen hundred years ago--the other day...light came out of this river since--you say knights? Yes; but it is like a running blaze on a plain, like a flash of lightning in the clouds. We live in the flicker--may it last as long as the old earth keeps rolling.*" She interrupts herself. Gets out of bed, grabs a pillow and starts slapping at the walls. "Bon, get up, catch it. *C'mon*," she says. I open an eye. She could be a model. "Oh, I hate them, help me catch them."

"They're not that bad," I say.

"I can't sleep if I know they're in here. C'mon, help me catch them."

"Do you have to smoke in bed?"

"It's my bed. God, I'll do what I want.

"Yes, alright, but I feel sick."

"What kind of sick?"

"Like a dull pain. Everything is difficult."

"Have you been to the doctor?" she asks.

"No," I say. "What for?" My hairy leg looks stupid next to hers.

"They can give you a blood test, see what the problem is."

"This always happens after a tour," I say. "I'm burnt out, that's all."

"Well, you won't sleep if there're mozzies in here," she says, "I'll keep you awake."

"Just ignore them, they'll go away."

"What and risk dengue fever, or meningitis? I've already got a bite on my thigh."

"Lucky mozzy," I say, taking a slurp of whisky from the bedside table. In my mind I see Malcolm looking up at me on the bus. I'm short of breath and powerless. She claps, and claps again.

"Little bastards, I hate them," she says.

"I hate you," I say.

"Bon, please. No need to speak like that." Her voice gets gravelly as she gets angry.

"Quick, get up, I caught a moth. I'm going to put it outside."

"Put it out yourself."

"I can't," she says, "if I move it to one hand I'll kill it."

"Don't kill it."

"*Well get up and open the window.*" She's really angry now. I don't answer. The pillow saves me from the charade. I hear the squeaking of the window handle. "Oh shit, see, it's flying around again." She jumps in bed, lies down with her back to me, pulling the blanket with her. "Good night," she says. I don't reply. After a few minutes and a few sighs, she says, "Don't go to sleep angry with me, it's not healthy." Reluctantly, I roll over and give her a peck and say goodnight. "You okay?" she asks, her eyes sympathetic.

"They're going to get rid of me," I say, a tightness rising.

"Who?"

'The band, I think they're gunna get another singer for America."

"They can't do that," she says, wide awake. "You virtually *are* the band. You write all the lyrics, come up with all the titles, do all the interviews."

"Hardly anyone reads the lyrics, Silver," I say. "They write all the riffs. It's Malcolm's baby."

"Oh." We're lying face to face, in a blanket-tent.

"The Yanks won't give me a visa, because of my drug conviction. The record company doesn't like me, and..."

"But you're nothing like how they portray you. The other day I saw an AC/DC poster that had the writing 'remove these posters and Bon will punch you in the face'. And I thought, Bon wouldn't punch anyone, especially over a bloody poster."

"I know, Browning comes up with all that stuff. He thinks it'll sell more records. They're not going to release *Dirty Deeds* in the States." I run my finger along her eyebrow. "I don't know if I can handle all this touring anymore. I've been sleeping in the back of vans for ten years. I'm burnt out. I'm losing my voice. The band's in big debt. All this touring costs a lot of money. Be a long time before I see any of it. They have to keep playing and recording, getting further and further in the red." Her eyes scan my face left and right. She kisses my fingers.

"I've been thinking," I say. "If you wanted to we could get married and have kids, ya know. We could buy a house. I'll get a steady job. I'll work at the fertiliser factory in Adelaide again, I don't care. I can play shows at night for a bit of pocket money. Bruce and I could start another band, easy." She closes her eyes, flips the blanket open and sits up. "We could live here and save up and buy an apartment and then rent it out and live in Australia for nothing. I'll help you until we get the money together." She puts her book on her bedside table. Once I've said these things it makes sense to me. I see a different future. She sits up and brings a flame to her white stick.

"Bon, you stupid bastard. I'm not working my guts out trying to get a deposit for a place," she says, exhaling a stream of smoke, "just to have it ruined by another bloody marriage. God."

"You could get your old job back at Adelaide uni," I say.

"I'm *not* going back to Adelaide, that's for sure, not while my sister is there."

"Sydney then...?"

"You know what happened in Sydney last time. Aren't you still married?" She puts the cigarette in the groove in the ashtray and gets up, wraps herself in a white robe.

"We're getting a divorce. Anywhere you want Silver, you know I love you. I'll do anything." She goes into the kitchen and puts the kettle on. She asks if I want a cup and starts doing the dishes. I lay in her warm patch. Outside the clouds have spots of blue and I can hear the street cleaners. I take a swig of whisky and feel the acid burn the lining of my empty stomach. Silver brings in a pot of tea and some cups on a tray.

"You know what I realised when I was travelling?" she asks. Her eyes are sad, like all the fight has gone out of her. "There are two types of people in the world. Adults trying to be children and children trying to be adults. You rarely meet people capable of being both. But you, Bon. You're like Peter Pan." She lets out a sigh and closes her eyes, her black hair spreads out on the bed. She mumbles to herself. She rolls over but her hair stays still.

I get up, go to the kitchen and cut a slice of bread. There's butter in the fridge but it's too hard, so I don't bother. I get dressed and roll myself a joint. I put a Lorraine Ellison album on and stare at the star painting, all these different thoughts going through my mind. My eyes blur with tears. I rip a sheet of paper out of a notebook and start scribbling.

THE PRESSURE BUILDS, THE STEAM ~~WHISTLE~~ BLOWS
A COLD HEART IN A BODY BAG, ~~ARE~~ IS LAYING LOW

WARMTH MISSING IN HER ~~NEIGHBOURHOOD~~ OVERCOAT
AND HER DRYING EYES

I SPEND MY WEEKENDS HIDING BURNT SPOONS
MADE ~~MY~~ COFFEE ~~WHISTLING~~ TO HER TUNE

SHOOTING UP, SHOOTING DOWN,
THERE IS NO ONE AROUND
GONE BLUESIN', MY LADY'S GONE BLUESIN'

A mozzie lands on the page and I slap it, blood oozing out. Since this is my last day with Atlantic I'll go to their office and borrow as many records as I can carry. I kiss Silver on the forehead, her skin soft, her nails red.

The air is thick and the footpath is still wet from the cleaners. The street looks the same left to right, lines and lines of terraces. I have to think twice about which way it is to the station. A tall man with his hands in pockets is singing to himself, *Hey, you, get-off-a-my-cloud.* I buy a little notebook and pen and a bottle of whisky. I'm thinking if I can write a few songs they might change their minds.

On the platform, dry, dead air whooshes before the train. I slip the notebook in my chest pocket and close my leather jacket and check myself in the window. I have time to kill. When we stop at St. James I see the sign for the museum and jump off. Up the steps and follow the long tunnel.

It's warm inside the museum. There are groups of school kids and oldies. Most of the statues and paintings don't do anything for me but one catches my eye. A naked woman made of white plaster. She has smooth skin and long hair.

"She's a beauty, isn't she?" asks the museum guard.

"She's a bit of alright, I guess, for a statue," I say. "I prefer the live ones."

"Oh, but Venus is the greatest of them all," he says. "*She* is the foam that binds ocean and earth. She is the waves that wash up the sand we build our sand castles from. The same waves that wash our castles away. The pillow that calms man and woman." His face is scrunched up trying to focus. "Her sexual appetite is inexhaustible. She would eat you for breakfast, old son," he scoffs, rising on his heels, proud of himself. I'm starting to like this geezer.

"Is that so?" I ask.

"One glance from her and you won't even so much as think of another woman for years. Yet, if you look close enough you can see her in every woman's eyes."

"Bloody hell, mate. She sounds like a handful. I know a few women like that." I stand a little further back and cross my arms.

"Yeah, she's a handful alright. It's shame she lost her arms."

"What happened there?"

"Found her like that when they dug her up, somewhere in Italy." He sounds happy as he says this.

"I kinda like her like that," I say. "She's more powerful." He walks to the front desk and starts chatting with someone else. I take out my notebook. I have to draw circles to get the pen working. At first I struggle to think of what to write, recalling what Bruce said in the hospital: no words ending with 'ING'.

IT WAS ONE OF THOSE DAYS WHEN
YOU CLEAR OUT THE HAZE
AND THERE'S ONLY ME AND THERE'S YOU
SHE ~~ISN'T~~ WASN'T THE VERSE, ~~ISN'T~~ WASN'T THE BLAST
WE KNEW WE WERE GETTIN' LOW
I WAS MORE THAN A MAN, WITH THIS WOMAN
LIKE A GOD CRASHED TO THE EARTH.

SHE TOUCHED ME TOO CLOSE.
A TOUCH TOO CLOSE.

SHE HAD HER HEAD AT AN ANGLE, ~~STROKING MY CHIN~~
A STATUE OF VENUS AT LARGE
STEALING MY DESIRE, SAPPING MY SIN

Oh shit. I've spent so long staring at Venus I've run out of time to go to Atlantic and pick up pick up some records. Just head straight to the band meeting instead. I go out into the dead calm London day. I take a narrow street and make my way to the river wall. I'm forced off my line by busy Londoners. A small stream flows inside the curb. A pub with green letters on the window. A quick dram? I press on my chest pocket, notebook still there.

I watch the brown sludge sprinkled with white plastic and off-white boats. The sky is sick smog-grey. Two swans take off like snooker balls bouncing from a break. Lights and bridges appear behind dark figures walking at me. A man in a suit is badgering a beggar, saying, "Remember my face, my wife has given you money every week for the last ten years, so don't ask me again." At a bend the river broadens and a great patch of mud expands below the wall. Holding back tears, I sing to myself. I lean on my elbows and watch someone in a raincoat and wellingtons pick through the mud and litter. They empty their bucket into a shopping trolley and don't once look up. A paddle steamer festooned with lights, like a powder room, struggles by, and I turn to face the music.

Malcolm and Angus' house has a concrete stoop that curves up to a white door with frosted glass above it. The light is on. I take a deep sigh and tap the brass bulb a few times. I turn my back to the door. Red buses move between houses with countless windows. I knock again and thrust my hands inside my jacket pockets. No answer. I go back down to street level next to the dented bins and look to the second floor. A rattle on the lock and then the door opens. The outline of Angus, short, shirtless, lean, shoulder length hair. He lifts the neck of his guitar up and steps outside, looks both ways up the street.

"Bon," he says, "how's it garn, mate? We're just having a blow." He leaves the door open and walks back up the hallway, telephone books and bills all over the carpet. I follow him into the kitchen. Malcolm sits in the middle of the floor, a serious look on his face. He has a dollop of jam on his cheek that Angus hasn't told him about.

"You wanna cup of tea?" asks Angus.

"Alright, yeah."

"Kettle's boiled, cups are in the cupboard."

"Whatchya been up to? asks Malcolm, not pausing his playing.

"Oh, ya know, walking around, writing some lyrics," I say. "Wanna see them?"

"Not right now," he says.

"Where's everyone else?" I ask.

"You're half an hour early," replies Angus, ejecting a cassette from the black recorder, flipping it over.

"Guess what we heard this arvo?" says Malcolm.

"What?" I take a sip of tea, blowing first and slurping deliberately.

"Browning says U.F.O. are looking for a new singer." I look up at the ceiling. There's a little bit of dandruff on my shoulder, I blow it off. This is the moment, let's get it over with.

"This is it then?" I ask, my hand checks for my notebook in my chest pocket.

"This is what?" says Angus.

"You're kicking me out?" I'm choking up a bit. Malcolm scrunches up his nose, frowns at Angus, looks me in the eye for a change, they're soft and tired.

"Are you crazy Bon? 'Course we're not kicking you out, you're one of us." My heart is pounding.

"There's a rumour going around that Atlantic want a different singer," I say.

"Fuck management," says Malcolm. "They never understood us in the first place. If they want blood, they've got it. We're finding a replacement for Mark, not you." I take out my small whiskey bottle and take a slurp, feeling relieved and confused at once.

"What's he done?" I ask.

"He just doesn't get it, Bon," says Malcolm. "We've gone up a level since we first came here. He's more of headache than we need if we're gunna go to the States."

"He never practices,' says Angus. "Never occurred to him to get bass or singing lessons."

"Why don't you tell—"

"We're trying to run a band here, not a kindergarten," says Malcolm.

"We found a bloke more your age," says Angus. "Remember the band called Home?"

"And Bandit?" asks Malcolm.

"Home rings a bell," I say. "They were kicking around when Fraternity were here."

"Yeh," says Malcolm, starting to act like the bloke I know. "The bass player from that band."

"What about Mark?" I ask.

"He's on his way over now. Him and Phil." I pull my jacket tight. Why did they drag me over here to kick him out? Mark's gunna think I helped plan all of this.

"Yous talked to him about it?"

"Given him enough chances," pipes up Angus. The door knocks and Angus gets up and lets them in. Phil stands in the doorway, his face as white as the door frame. I cross my arms and catch Mark's eyes and let him know I'm not into what's going down.

Malcolm stands up, crosses his arms like everyone else, and says, "There's no easy way to say this, but we're gunna have to let you go, Mark. It's not working out."

Mark looks out the kitchen window, shakes his head, frowns, clenches his fist, goes to speak, stops and goes to speak again. "You all decided this, did yas?' he says. No-one speaks. I can hear Mark breathing. He looks at all of us, one by one. "Well, you're all so fucking heroic but none of you can talk?"

"It's nothing personal Mark," I say. "You're a great bass player—"

"We want someone who can sing backing vocals," says Malcolm. "That's all..." Mark looks like he's gunna punch him out.

"I can. I'll... What if. How about? If..." says Mark. There's another long pause and then Mark looks out the window again, his hands are trembling and he shakes his head in disbelief and then says, "If that's what you guys want." He looks over to Phil who shrugs his shoulders.

"C'mon Mark," says Phil. "I'll get a taxi with you."

BAD BOY BOOGIE
NEW YORK -- 1979

I wake up nervous, hot and sweaty. You'd think the nerves would go away. Ten times I wake up and the bed is empty. Adrenaline wakes me up. High temperature. Still wired from last night's gig. All those happy faces blown back.

Ideas for songs wake me up. Suzy wakes me up. Her cool drive. Irene wakes me up. Her warm affection, her easy friendship makes me toss and turn. Silver wakes me up. Her smart conversation, her intellect. Lines, images, my fuck-ups wake me and I cannot go back to sleep. There's drool on the pillow and the daylight glow from behind the blind. The phone rings.

"How you doin, Bon? Neeup." It's Angus, he's in the next room. I go to talk but no sound comes out. I clear my throat into the receiver to annoy him. "Okay, just having a hand shandy, how are ya?"

"You sound like shit, mate."

"Thanks, Angus, you try singing every night."

"Yeah, I can hardly walk. Some show last night, you meet the girl with the missing nipples?"

"*Meet* her? She's here with me. My hotel room was full of naked women when I got in. Took me a few hours to kick them out. You know what they're like."

"Yeah right, Bon. We'll come by in a few hours to pick you up. Got a surprise for ya."

"What time is it in Australia?"

"How the fuck would I know?" I hear him slurp a cup of tea. "See ya later, crocodile."

I open the blind. Light whooshes in, everything is brown. Brown walls, brown bed, brown table, brown bathroom. I feel like I'm inside a big turd. An air vent hums. Can't open the window. The view is straight out to a brick wall. I ring reception and ask them to bring breakfast. I take out a postcard of the Statue of Liberty and start writing.

DEAR SUZY,

I'M IN MY UNDIES IN A HOTEL. WE'RE OUT ON THE ROAD SUPPORTING KISS. THEY BLOW US OFF THE STAGE EVERY NIGHT. THAT'S WHAT THEY TELL US. THIS TOUR IS 100 DATES IN JUST ABOUT AS MANY DAYS. I FEEL LIKE A TEN YEAR OLD SHOE THAT'S GOT NO SOLE. OR SOUL MATE. AFTER THE STATES WE FLY BACK TO LONDON FOR A HANDFUL OF SHOWS AND TO RECORD THEN BACK TO SYDNEY. WILL YOU BE IN PERTH AT CHRISTMAS?

THE OTHER NIGHT PHIL AND I DECIDED TO CLIMB THE STATUE OF LIBERTY. LOOKS CLOSE FROM YOUR HOTEL ROOM. TAKES US AN HOUR TO GET THERE AND WE PAY TO GET IN BUT THE LIFT IS BROKEN. TAKES ANOTHER 30 MINS TO CLIMB HER. WE'RE UP WHERE THE FLAMES SHOULD BE COMING OUT SO WE HAVE A JAZZ CIGARETTE AND PRETEND THE SMOKE IS COMING OUT THE TORCH.

ANYWAY, IT GETS DARK AND WE CLIMB BACK DOWN AND

THE GUARD IS ASKING HOW WE GOT INSIDE. HE WAS ABOUT TO LOCK UP. WOULD HAVE BEEN PRETTY FUNNY TO BE LOCKED INSIDE THE STATUE OF LIBERTY. AS YOU CAN SEE, LIFE SURE AIN'T DULL. ANYWAY LOVE, SEE YOU IN PERTH,

BON XO.

Breakfast arrives. Bacon, eggs, coffee and hash browns. Don't know why they're called hash browns. New York, what a hell hole. When we drove in from the airport our taxis were attacked. You can't tell the difference between cloud and fog. Sunlight doesn't penetrate, just a peach coloured ring overhead, and that's if you can get out of the building shade. Been dreaming about coming here for years. What a let down. All the streets are dirty, rubbish everywhere. I have to be inside. Outside I can hardly breathe. Kills my throat.

I mix up my throat soothing concoction of warmed red wine, honey and a little salt. A glass with breakfast and another after to make sure. Gurgle that down. New York, you're either in air conditioning, or in smog. Try walking around at night without being stabbed. The big rotten apple.

I shave and get dressed and go to the lobby and send my letter off. I ask the concierge if he knows anywhere I can get my throat looked at. He says he knows a great acupuncturist around the corner. Says he'll cure anything.

"What about a basketball stuck in your throat?" I ask. "Anything," he says. "Turn the corner on West 57th Street."

One thing you gotta give New York is the people. Ten in the morning, guys busking, hustling, doing card tricks. Fruit vendors, news stands, hot dog men, all wise guys. Chaos. I find the place out the back of a mini-mart. An anatomy picture on the door with the label, 'W.L. Chang - Acupuncturist'. A small Chinese man in a white robe opens the door, grabs me by the elbow and leads me into one of the rooms.

"What's your name, sir?"

"Bon, Bon Scott."

"Age?"

"Thirty three."

"Occupation?"

"Singer. I got this sore thro..." He asks a few more questions, leans over and takes my hand, turns it over and looks closely at my nails. He says to poke my tongue out, turn my head up to the light. He takes my pulse, looks in my eyes. He makes a note. His skin is clear and soft, his veins visible. He says to go into the next room, strip to my underwear and lie on the bed, face up. Lucky I wore undies today. I pull one of the towels over my balls and lie back and close my eyes.

Mr Chang enters the room and says to try to relax. A few moments later the warm feeling of a sponge and then a little pin prick. He's poking all around my belly and chest. One of the needles feels weird and when I tell him he moves it. He takes the needles out and tells me to roll over.

"My throat," I say. "It's my throat."

"Yes, Mister Scott, but your insides are rotten. You have insides of sixty year old man. I cannot fix your throat until liver and kidney fixed. Very serious." I give in and try to relax. Somehow, the taste of bourbon and Coke fills my mouth.

"You have asthma, Mr Scott?" he asks, poking a pin in the side of my neck.

"Yes." This guy is good.

"Oh, very serious." My pendant necklace from Silver dangles in front of me, I rub it. He tells me to lie still. I start to feel better, looser, more energy. My throat feels a bit better. He takes the remaining pins out and tells me to take my time and get dressed.

I open the door and he's in his office. I roll my shoulders, open my wallet and pay. He doesn't look at me.

"You make another appointment?"

"I'm leaving town in a few days."

"You come in tomorrow?" I buy a soda water and walk back to the hotel through Central Park. Overcast and muggy. Don't know if the itchiness is a reaction to the pins, or the humidity. Joggers crunch the paths. Dogs sniff at the base of trees. Workers scoop up piles of leaves. An image of Dad comes in a flicker. We're in Kerriemuir, burning leaves in the back yard. He picks me up and we watch the flames.

Maybe I'll stop drinking. In a big lake I see a small remote control yacht. Must be Phil. He has all these toys in his hotel room. Cars, helicopters, airplanes and yachts. He's wearing blue jeans and a white shirt. His jacket lays over a bollard near a little tool kit, packet of cigarettes and a sandwich with one bite out of it. He stands outside a faint line of shade. The little boat is heading straight for us. He steers it in and picks it up by the bottom like a fish.

"Bloody thing keeps leaking," he says, one eye closed in the glare. He has dark rings under his eyes. He fidgets with a small plug, empties the water and puts the boat back in. The white toy moves away. He comes over and lights a cigarette, wiping his nose. Cocaine. He catches himself wiping and looks at me. His gentle eyes have changed.

"Get much sleep?" I ask him.

"Why?"

"Just wondering. I got up at six, couldn't go back to sleep for two hours, then woke up again at nine."

"What are you trying to say? I don't sleep enough?"

"No. I was just wondering."

"Yeah, well. Don't worry about me. You worry about yourself."

"Just went to the doctor," I tell him. "Says everything's good. Fighting fit."

"Lucky you."

"Says I should slow down on the drinking though."

"Heard that before."

"You know, you don't have to drive the bus anymore, we can afford a driver."

"That's not what Malcolm said." He clutches his nose with thumb and finger. "They won't kick me out if I do both jobs, will they? I like driving. What's your problem?"

"They won't kick you out Phil, but if you're too fucked to play, they might have to kick you out."

"Who are you, the band manager? Why are you worried about me all of a sudden? Go find someone else to pick on." He turns his back on me. A woman runs by, her blonde pony tail swings from side to side. Phil keeps fidgeting with his yacht, sending it back out into the water. For a few moments the sun pokes through the clouds.

"What do think of Cliff?" he asks.

"He can play bass alright. I like him."

"You like everyone."

"He's bloody smooth." I wrack my brain for something else to say, nothing comes. I stand up and wipe some dirt from my bum. "I'll see you at Atlantic later then," I say.

"See you on the bus?"

"We taking the bus? I though we were getting taxis?"

"Ahmet Ertegun's meant to be there, a gold platinum thingy presentation," says Phil. I wipe the sand off my bum and I walk a few yards. "Hey Bon," he yells.

"What?"

"Get fucked," he smiles. In the cool of the trees my stomach rumbles and I feel like a ghost.

We get off the bus at the back of Atlantic. A big white building, recording studio, radio station, auditorium, offices all in one. We're ushered up stairs to the president's suite by some sexy secretary. The office is lined with framed gold records. There's a couple of couches and Ahmet Ertegun's desk. A bar off to one side. We all sit down and he walks in from the dunny door.

"Gentlemen," he says. "Welcome to Atlantic." He raises his arms out wide and then claps them together. We all stand up to shake his hand. Some photographer snaps away. He has a tanned bald head, rimmed circle glasses over big brown eyes that look straight through you. His mo and goatee cover his lips so when he speaks it's all sound and no movement. He wears a white shirt with a white tie and dinner jacket.

"Please, sit," he says, waving his hands. "How is New York treating you? Isn't it wonderful"

"We haven't really had..." Angus starts to say.

"Oh, Monica, yes, bring them over dear." A woman enters with the framed records. She awkwardly passes them to Ahmet.

"Gentlemen, it is with great pleasure I present to you the gold record for five hundred thousand sales of *Highway to Hell* in America."

"I think I sold nearly four hundred thousand of those myself," says Angus. We all laugh.

"Yeah, and I sold the other one hundred thousand," says Phil.

"Well, it wasn't Atlantic that sold them, that's for sure" I add, joining the wind up. Ahmet's laugh turns to a frown instantly.

"Boys, please, is something the matter?"

"We just wanna be able to buy some guitar strings, tha's all," says Malcolm. Monica enters the room again, this time with two bottles of champagne on a tray. She passes one to Ahmet, puts the other on his desk, and collects some glasses from the sideboard.

"You haven't got any guitar strings?"

"I've been on the same set for two years, man," says Angus. "I take them off and boil them to get the sweat out." He sniffs and turns away to hide his laughter. Phil grabs the other bottle and starts to unwind the top.

"I got holes in my shoes. I got holes in my jeans," I say. Ahmet stops opening his bottle and looks at us seriously.

"You mean to tell me you haven't received the money allocated to you for the tour?"

"Be nice to have an amp that works," says Angus.

"No point driving around in a limo if your microphones don't work," I say, piling on the bullshit.

"I went to the guitar shop the other day," says Angus. "I said to the guy, I want a thirty inch speaker. He says they don't make them. I said, okay, I want thirty one inch speakers in a cabinet. He says they don't make them. I said I want a guitar with four necks, he says they don't make them. Fucking America." He starts to smile and we all start laughing and Ahmet begins to get we're pulling the piss. His shoulders relax and he starts laughing and pouring drinks, the bubbles spilling over. He offers me a glass and I hesitate.

"Oh, come on, one glass won't kill you. Call yourself a rock and roll star?"

"I never drink before a show," I say. Phil gives me a look.

"You don't wanna get Bon started," says Malcolm. Angus refuses a glass too. Ahmet looks surprised.

"Well, I respect that..."

"Oh give me a glass then" I say. I swish the fruity bitterness around my mouth.

"You fellas should know," says Ahmet, "we spent a lot of money on you guys. We're hoping for bigger things. We're not out of the woods yet."

"Don't you worry about us," interjects Malcolm. "We're gunna be the biggest band in the world. Bigger than...what's their name?"

"Led Zeppelin?"

"Nah, bigger than them."

"The Beatles?"

"They're finished anyway," I say.

"The Rolling Stones? Bigger than The Rolling Stones," adds Malcolm, finishing his glass and pouring another.

"I sure hope so, for all of our benefits," says Ahmet, sitting on the front of his desk. "You work harder than any band I know. The kids in America take to you. You know, I listened to your previous record the other day. *Powerage*. Some good shit. You boys have the musical depth and that means a lot to me. The simpler the better, when it comes to blues."

"The next one's gunna be simpler and better yet," says

Malcolm. "You wait. We're working some of the songs out now, and we'll go into the studio with Mutt in what," he looks at Angus and me, "March or April?"

"If we don't die from malnutrition and exhaustion before then," I quip.

"I hear he's a bit of a wizard in the studio, this Mutt fella," says Ahmet, lacing his hands together over his balls.

"Robert Mutt Langer, he's a genius that cunt," I say.

"*What a cunt*," says Phil, smiling.

"Excuse me," says Ahmet, his white teeth showing. "Oh, you Australians say *cunt* a lot, don't you?"

"We're not Australian, we're Scottish," says Malcolm.

"Gentlemen, let me say this, if I can. We're now ready to take you to the big time. That means we're not going to be holding anything back. We're going to use all of our muscle to get you on every radio and television station in the country. If they won't play your record, we'll pay them to play your record. Everyone has a price. Your name will be on everyone's lips."

"That's what you guys said twelve months ago," says Angus, his upper lip curling. "You didn't even release *Dirty Deeds* here."

"Well, I wasn't aware of that. Listen. This business can change in a second. Don't be naive and think you can just do whatever you want whenever you want. We're not the bad guys. We're on your side. Whatever happened between AC/DC and Atlantic is all water under the bridge. I haven't seen a hard hitting band like you guys for a long time. You blow my mind. Angus is hilarious, even when his pants go missing. So, please, fellas, take it from me personally. Malcolm, if you have any problems, you ring me directly."

"Yeah, I wanna talk to you," says Malcolm. They both walk out of earshot, chatting.

Phil and Cliff chat away finishing the champagne. Angus, dressed in his school uniform, holding the neck of his SG, sits next to me on the couch. For once he doesn't play his guitar. He looks up at the ceiling. He wiggles about. He puts his feet on the coffee table, takes them off.

"Alright, Bon?" He puts out a cigarette and lights another one.

"Something on your mind mate?"

"No. What makes you say that?"

"Nothing in particular."

"It's just...just," he takes a long drag of his fag.

"Spit it out, Angus."

"Chicks mate. It's the chicks, they do my head in."

"You mean you don't know what to do with your old fella?"

"No. Yeah, there's that, but, as well, there's just so many of them. They come backstage and rip my clothes off. I try to hide but they always find me. Problem with these American birds is they don't even know the lyrics."

"Don't ask me Angus, I've been with hundreds of women, there's no trick, you just take what comes your way. If you arrive at the party too early, so what? There'll be another party in twenty minutes. The girls love it, that's all you need to remember. No one is forcing them to be backstage or anywhere with you."

"But they do my head in, Bon. They'll ask you for a glass of water, and when you say there's a jug of water over there they get all upset."

"Some of them will play games," I say, rubbing my chin. "You just battle on, tell them what they want to hear. Works, usually. We can always hit the road."

He clutches his face and wipes the snot out of his nose with thumb and forefinger. He frowns, and then looks across my line of vision focusing on a bin in the corner.

"Imagine if everyone saw everyone else the way doctors see everyone. What do they call it? Objective?" He's starting one of his rants. "Men and women walking down the street naked, not a care in the world. But doctors are the only people who wanna have sex. So when you get sick, doctors can't keep their hands off you, dirty bastards. You go in for a check up and the docs are humping your leg like a Jack Russell."

"It'd be a bit weird, Angus. Everyone would want to be a doctor." He laughs.

"Imagine on a plane or in a restaurant, some poor bugger's got heart problems, you'll have about twenty people scrambling to root the poor bugger," he says.

"Thing is, Angus, women have it sorted. They're wired differently. A hundred thousand years ago, or whenever it happened, men were walking around with no shirts on, their lollie bags dangling in the wind, women pretending not to notice. So now blokes walk around with their shirts off all the time. A woman takes her shirt off and blokes are drooling and carrying on."

"I met this girl, Ellen," he says, "I really like her."

"Don't ask me about love, Angus. I haven't got a clue. Two speeding trains heading toward one another only have to miss by an inch."

"*What?*" he asks.

"Exactly mate. Don't ask me. I've been married. I can't even get divorced. I love Silver, but she left me. I hope rock and roll never leaves me... So, when do I get to meet her?"

"Who?" He starts playing a few scales.

"This girl, Ellen."

"Oh, she's coming to the show tonight."

"Where's my surprise?"

"What surprise?"

"You said on the phone this morning you had a surprise."

"Ah yeah, that. We got you a remote microphone, like my guitar."

"I heard they go flat a lot, more than guitars."

"Yeah, we got you three, to swap between songs."

Malcolm returns and Ahmet says goodbye and we're taken

downstairs to the backstage area. You can hear the crowd through the big black curtains. The drum kit, amps and microphones are all set up by our roadies. An assistant comes up and says we're on in five minutes. I take a few big gulps of cough medicine and some pain killers. Malcolm calls me over and we gather around in something like a huddle. We've never huddled before. Phil leans in. Cliff leans in.

"Okay," says Malcolm, "this is it. Angus and I have been thinking, we wanna do a stage act in *Bad Boy Boogie*. In the middle part he's gunna do a little dance and provoke the audience and do a moonie at them. We then go back into the song with the crescendo as normal."

"You still want me to do the bass line?" asks Cliff.

"Yeah, you do the build up exactly the same, but later. You'll know when."

"So it's the same, but Angus drops his dacks?" asks Phil.

"Yeah," say Angus and Malcolm at the same time. We take to the stage one by one. Phil first, then Cliff, Malcolm, then Angus. The house is packed with about a thousand people. The suited announcer stands at the microphone.

"Good evening ladies and gentlemen, I'm Ed Sciaky, welcoming you all to the world famous Atlantic Recording Studios in New York City for a first in a series of live radio concerts." The crowd cheers. "Please welcome, A-C-D-C."

Cliff starts with the rumbling intro, his bass pulsing in and out. The new remote microphone feels strange. I talk to the audience. "Can I have your attention please? We are live on air, and we'd like your participation. This is a song for ya, called *Live Wire.*" The guy at the desk lifts my volume half way through my intro. One of these strange afternoon shows when the audience is sober. Have to work even harder. I warm my voice up, "*Hell yeah, LIVE WIRE BABY.*"

Malc and Angus crank the opening chords and we are away. Angus and I point at the kids in the crowd. We don't shy away from them anymore. If we can get them to give us a finger or a 'Fuck you.' Our work has begun. The song finishes. "Thank you very much, we'll melt the ice huh?" I say. The feeling of death dissipating.

Streams of smoke jet up quickly out of the audience and form a cloud in the auditorium. I rip my denim jacket off, my jeans are tight. The pain disappears once we get warmed up. Lately I've been doing what I call shape shifting. I dance a different style for each song. *Problem Child,* I'm a boxer. *Highway to Hell,* I'm a crow on a post. *Sin City,* I'm a snake. *Rocker,* I'm a crab. As soon as the song finishes the crowd start chanting ANGUS, ANGUS, ANGUS, fitting in neatly with the intro to *Whole Lotta Rosie.*

Bad Boy Boogie begins with Angus slowly, ever so slowly, bending his light strings. The lights lower and turn red. He quickens the alternating notes letting the last note ring out then raising his ear to the audience until they cheer in recognition. He nods in agreement. This song, when we get it right, is the greatest song in rock and roll history and if anyone wants to disagree with me I'll punch them out. Anyone who says otherwise hasn't stood in the front row, closed their eyes and let the song move through them.

Angus falls on his back and spins around like a poisoned cockroach. His feet flick up. He gets up and runs around in circles playing furiously in a haze of overdriven drones-come -blues-mixed-licks. He raises his right hand to the audience. Louder cheers. A circle of sweat seeps through the back of his felt school blazer.

I look at Malcolm and he's in total concentration, his right leg tapping. Cliff hides behind his mop of hair, a wall of bass cabinets behind him. Angus drops his shoulders as two shadows follow him to the front of the Marshall stacks, the guitar starts to feedback. A high pitched squeal wavers in the air. The battle between the crowd cheers and the amp volume goes on. Phil counts us in with the hi-hat. 1...2...1-2-3-4, full throttle to the engines, BANG-BANG-BANG-BANG like gun shots.

I do my own version of the Chuck Berry duck walk and rip the crotch of my jeans. A little wink to the girls up the front. We play faster than the album version. Phil is off the chain. Malcolm keeps up easily. The lights flash. First verse, second verse, chorus. I raise my voice and jump octaves. The opposites roll off my tongue. The chorus ends, the break down begins, bass and bass drum like a heart beat, DOOF-DOOF. The volume lowers slowly.

Angus keeps the same high note going and Phil, Malcolm and Cliff syncopate the rhythm. I run my hand through my hair and shake in anticipation. I go to the front of the stage and ask the audience to clap to the beat. Malcolm and Cliff tease the audience with a fake build up, Phil rim hits the snare. Silence. Tease. Loud cheer.

I go back stage and find my cough syrup. Angus starts to taunt the crowd. He hands his guitar to a roadie. He pries his tie off, twirls it in front of him and throws it off the front of the stage. Jeers. He takes off his jacket, pulls it through his legs and pretends to wank the sleeve. He unbuttons his shirt showing his tiny torso. He pulls the front of his shorts out and points to his dick. His dumb face is perfect. The crowd cheers. Crash from the cymbals.

He lowers his arms as if patting the crowd quiet and Malcolm and Cliff lower their volume. He climbs the front of the drum riser and turns his back to the crowd. He unbuttons his shorts. With a short drum roll he quickly flashes his bare bum to the crowd. They throw rubbish on stage in disgust. Angus bows and straps his guitar back on.

I have a few moments to rest while I'm watching. I wipe my face with a towel and take a few hits from my asthma puffer. You know how a certain song reminds you of a place? Even if that place has nothing to do with the song? *Bad Boy Boogie* always reminds me of Riverbank. The cell and the beds and the books and Norman's face and his hands and feet on the walls. The planes taking off, the engines roaring. The mosquitos buzzing as I try to sleep. Monkey and his black boots. I compare the engine noise to the sound of the band getting louder and louder and louder. The skin on your face starts to ripple. I nod to my imaginary Norman, wherever he is.

The best band in the world playing our best song. And I'm in it! We blues out and begin the slow creep up to the climax, the jet engines accelerating. The bass moves up the neck getting faster and faster. The drums hammer in with the rhythm guitar that grows louder and looser then Phil opens the hi-hat, Angus letting the feedback blast through his single note, the frequencies filling up until there's no room left, we take off and I re-enter the stage and take a deep breath and sing, *"I won't tell you a story, tell you no lie,"* and we are off the ground. The crowd cheers loud and hysterical. Their happy faces look up to us. We shake their hands and thank them. Angus' guitar sound still swirls as we all walk off stage to the back of the building.

I'm ready to collapse. I slink away to the green room, turn the main lights off and lie on the couch. I rub around my eyes and squeeze the top of my nose to try to get some air in, to break up the sinuses. I suck on the puffer a few times. I've forgotten to give the cordless microphone back to the roadies. There's a knock at the door. I wish I'd locked it now. A man enters and starts helping himself to booze and sandwiches. He talks to himself but I can't make out what he's saying.

"Who's that?" He jumps, puts his hand over his heart.

"Oh fuck. Jesus. Fuck. You scared the living daylights out of me." He leers in. "Ron? Is that you, Ron?"

"No, it's the Queen's mother."

"Ron, it's Vince, how the fuck are ya mate?"

"Vince, you cunt, what are you doing here?"

"Here with the ABC, doing a music documentary." He alters

his voice to make it sound like he's on the radio, "*Music to the World.*" I heard you caught up with Bruce and the boys in Adelaide, sorry I missed you man, I was in Melbourne organising this doco. So good to see ya mate. I've got some coke. You want some? We got a sweet allowance from the ABC, but Paul, the producer, is as straight as, so I got away from him for the night, when I heard you guys were playing I got here lickety split."

"I know Paul, he did the Long Way..." I try to get a word in. He starts chopping on the table with his credit card.

"You probably get offered this stuff all the time being a famous rock and roll star, hardly get it back home anymore. How's Angus and Malcolm these days, still little pricks who won't give you the time of day? They can play great but they're little assholes, I tell ya, I said hello to them outside and they didn't even recognise me. Saw George in Sydney recently, he's the same. Whole family's fucked... The missus sends her love by the way, oh mate you haven't even met my kid yet, Jesus mate, she's so beautiful, but I tell you what, it's good to get out of Australia, backwards shit hole." He rolls up a note.

"It's not that bad," I say, my voice croaky.

"Alright for you, mister rock and roll star, you get to come and go all the time." He sucks up a line, throws his head back, talks like he's holding his breath. "See some of the girls in the audience? Oh man, I could go a fuck right now." He takes a swig of whisky from the bottle he's pinched.

"What about your wife and kids?" I ask him.

"Fucking little Bonnie, always the romantic." He messes my hair up. "What's got into you mate, you sad or something? Don't you worry, Uncle Vince is here now. Party time." He claps his hand and stands up. "Have a line, mate."

"No thanks."

"Have a drink of this then. Come on, let's party."

"We've got another show later, at Madison Square Garden."

"Oh sweet, can you get me tickets? Isn't this great, Bon?

Whoever thought we'd end up in New York, me and you, the old gang. If those losers in Perth could see us now mate, what a trip man." The door opens and Malcolm walks in, grabs himself a beer, changes his shirt and washes his face.

"Hey Malcolm, great show man, great show," says Vince. "You guys are great, you really are."

"Eh Bon, you wanna turn that microphone off?" says Malcolm. "Everyone can hear you two out there."

"Oh shit," says Vince, picking the mike up off the table, switching it off. "I didn't mean any harm Malcolm, you know me mate, just kidding around."

"Don't matter," says Malcolm. "We're outta here in twenty, Bon." Malcolm leaves the room. Vince turns to me with his eyebrows raised.

"He doesn't fuck around, does he?"

"What time is it in Australia?" I ask him.

"Ummm, well, it's a quarter to six here, so about five in the morning in Adelaide. Why?"

"I wanna ring Irene."

"She's in Melbourne now mate, she's pregnant and everything."

"Really?"

"Dead set." A burning sensation pulses through my heart.

"You know who else is pregnant?" I ask him.

"Who?"

"Suzy. I caught up with her in Perth."

"That bitch, mate. I told you a thousand times to forget about her. Remember when she accused me of cracking onto her in rehearsals that time? She's full of it."

We pile in the bus and drive to Madison Square Garden and I take the opportunity to tape my jeans up. Takes about two hours in the traffic creeping over the bridge, but luckily Mork and Mindy are on the television. We get to the venue and again I hear a rumour that the singer in KISS thinks I can't sing and my voice will give out any moment and I think, *Fuck them, this has to stop.* They wanna bag us behind our back, they can deal with me personally. So Malc and I find their room, he loves a bit of biff. When we storm inside they're doing all kinds of stretches and warming up and I say a polite, *Hello,* to Gene putting his make up on and I go up to Ace who has a woman on each arm and I say, "What's this crap I keep hearing about you saying I can't sing and you guys think we're shit?" and he starts denying everything, pretending like he doesn't know what I'm talking about. This gets me real pissed off and I cock my fist to punch him in the face and he cowers and says, *Bon, Bon, Bon,* and no-one even tries to stop me, I look him in the eyes and I see the truth but I'm still pissed off and I kick the chair and then the lamp and immediately I think, *Shit, I've broken my toe,* but I don't show any pain, instead I start laughing and everyone else starts laughing but it hurts like hell and I'm just laughing from the pain, this bunch of sissies can't fight and it would be unfair for me to go for them as they'd end up in hospital, so I apologise to the ladies and go back to my room and Malc doesn't say anything, just starts tuning his guitar and I take my shoe off and my big toenail is shattered and blood has started seeping through my sock and gushing out the sides of my toenail and I get some ice out of the esky and a plastic bag and try to ice the swelling as we're on in half an hour. I might have to do this set bare foot but then they'll know my foot is busted so no, wrap some bandages and take some painkillers and a few slugs of my puffer and some more cough medicine and time to hit the stage another ten thousand kids as soon as we start we blow KISS off the stage once more, the sissies.

At the end of our set I don't wait for Angus to finish running from side to side and up and across the stage. I walk straight backstage and find the bus and enter and lie down. I'm fucked. Rooted. I need sleep. Shivering bad. Oh god, shivering, cold, heart pumping, ears ringing. Need to relax. I am a ghost. In the moisture on the window I finger the letters, H-E-L-L. I run the wet finger over my lips and forehead. So tired. My blood feels heavy and thick. Maybe a drink will fix this? No, better not. Water. I'm nearly asleep when Angus and a girl enter the bus and turn the radio on.

"Shut the door," I tell them. "Keep the cold out."

"It's fucking freezing in here anyway, Bon," says Angus. "This is the girl I was telling you about, Ellen." She stands over me, her face dark with the light behind her. I pull my arm out of the blanket and we shake hands.

"You are cold," she says, in a strong Dutch accent.

"Give me a chance," I reply, "you only just met me."

She frowns and says, "No, I mean your hand is cold."

"Don't worry about Bon, he's tough as," says Angus. She grabs another blanket from the back of the bus and lays it over me. I like her already. I grab the bottle of cough mixture and swig the bitter ooze. They lie in the next bed and start giggling and kissing and being in love. On the radio I hear, *Hi, I'm Allan Handelman and you're listening to The Allan Handelman Show. Coming up, we're talking to Bon Scott from an interview recorded last week in Atlanta.*

"Turn it off," I say.

"No, I want to listen," says Ellen.

Angus says, "Bon does all our interviews, don't you, Bon?" I prop my head up and pull the blanket around my feet. My toe still throbbing.

"If I can talk," I say. Ellen turns the radio up.

Handelman: When AC/DC started back in '76, what was the music situation like?

Me: Bad. Real Bad. I sound horrible. "Turn it off, Angus."

Handelman: For example?

Me: Well. We played our own style of music. The kind of music that everyone was into were things like ABBA. And Neil Diamond like, you know. That ilk of crap, you know.

Handelman: What gave you guys the incentive, or should I say the insight to know that up the road, two or three years, across the country, across the world, that your music would start vibrating, start getting people happy?

Me: Because, because, the people like rock and roll. I'm talking the people like, in general. I guess I'm talking mainly about people who are like ourselves who are lower middle class, upper working class, lower working class, whatever, you know. We just did what we liked and we figured that we're not dumb, and there's a whole lot of other people who like the same thing we like. At the time the radio stations were pushing this um, Linda Ronstadt, James Taylor crap, you know. I heard some radio station in the mid-west go: "and now the rock music without the noise." And played James Taylor.

Ellen's bracelets clack. Handelman sounds so enthusiastic. I sound drunk. I look out the window. The HELL letters are starting to blur together. A long line of cars bumper to bumper. The figures of people walking through headlight fog and exhaust fumes. The after show excitement I wish I could be part of.

Me: Rock and roll was staged in 1939, between then and 1945. It went through a crisis in the 60's, that's history.

My chest heaves quickly with short cat-like breaths. I'm a wuss. Whenever I get a cold I want to be looked after. Lie in bed and drink lemonade and eat Mum's chicken soup. I tune back into the interview.

Handelman: Let me ask you some more questions, you're doing so well. Can I ask about the song Let There Be Rock*? Now that's a religious song to a lot of people.*

Me: Well. It was to me, because I come up with the title about two years ago, Let There Be Rock, *and everyone went agh yeah great title, ya know, but what do we write* Let There Be Rock *about? ya know. So I went down to, right underneath the recording studio there's a book shop. And I bought a bible. I bought a bible. Don't let that soil my career, please. But I bought this bible. Put the book of Genesis, you know, "In the beginning" I thought fuck what a great title, what a great start to a song, "In the beginning" you know. It's just like that Rod Stewart song. Rod Stewart did that song* Wake Up Maggie *and the opening line is just so strong it just has to grab your attention, you know. The rest can be literally shit, the first line was like, "in the beginning" but then the brain wave, the second verse, "but it came to pass."*

My mother's a Christian, she's a lovely lady and she's a Christian and she goes to church every Sunday. She says, "Someone's gotta pray for ya."

An image of Carols by Candlelight comes to mind. Me, Mum and Dad, Dereck and Graeme in Fremantle, on Monument Hill. Mum has fruit cake.

Handelman: Has she heard your music recently? Has she put one of your records on her record player?

Me: She heard the new album. She has them all. Before the new album came out, she rang me. She says "oh yeah, what's it called?" I said: Highway to Hell. HAHA. She said "Trust you".

I try to piece together what happened last time I was home.

Dereck and Dad and I were drinking on the front verandah, looking out over the river. Remember playing with the next door neighbour's cat. Then Terry came over and we went into Fremantle and drank. I shake my head when I think about what I might have done. I can't remember. I feel so stupid.

"What did you do today?" Angus asks Ellen.

"Oh, I went to watch the space movie, the two thousand and one, one. It was very long. The apes were funny."

Handelman: Right. What was the feeling with the ABBA craze in Australia?

Me: ABBA had like five hit records in the top ten within the period of a month. In Australia, they did a tour there and they sold out. They must have made millions touring Australia. They played one concert that holds maybe 100,000 people. And they had tickets, like you could buy your air ticket, two nights in the hotel and your flight back for $150. Of which about seventy went to ABBA. Australia was the first place in the whole world that ABBA broke top ten-wise and they still haven't broken in America. I think they're kind of finished.

Handelman: In my opinion they have a nice style, but they're so overproduced. So LALALALALA.

Me: Well Australia's a kind of susceptible country. Even a few people like us are. HAHA.

Handelman: Do you feel that you would be compatible, or like you could live in this country? Do you feel like you get along with the people here?

Me: Well. I am going to live here. I'm going to buy a house up in North California. I mean, ya know, it's America. No more need be said. It's America.

"I didn't know you were going to live in North California," says Angus.

"Neither does my mother," I say. "She think's I'm going to live in fucking Spearwood."

"Where's that?" asks Ellen.

"A paddock near Fremantle," I say.

"What's wrong with that?" she asks.

"The country is beautiful, but the people are fucked," says Angus. "They kicked us out last time we were there."

"What for?"

"Flashing his arse everywhere," I say. Another swig of medicine. I roll over and put the pillow over my head. I wake again when the bus engine starts, the rumble shakes my bones and muscles.

Back at the hotel, staring at the brick wall. In my bag is my new compendium, I pull it out and write Irene a letter.

DEAR RENE,

I'M GOING THROUGH A BAD PATCH RIGHT NOW. HOPE YOU CAN HANDLE A SOPPY LETTER. CAN'T BE WITH ANYBODY BECAUSE I'M ALWAYS TOURING AND NEVER ANYWHERE LONG ENOUGH AND THEN THERE'S COUNTLESS WOMEN I CAN FUCK BUT I DON'T WANT THAT EITHER. WHAT'S THE MATTER WITH ME? NEED TO BE ON THE ROAD TO KEEP MY MIND BUSY. IM AN ALCO AGAIN AND NEED WEED TO SETTLE MY NERVES. SOMETIMES I THINK MORE MONEY WILL SOLVE ALL MY PROBLEMS. I JUST WANNA BE SOMEONE, YOU KNOW. THAT WAY WHEN I GET TALKED ABOUT IT'S GOOD. THAT'S ALL I WANT. BUT RIGHT NOW I NEED A FRIEND.

BON.

HIGHWAY TO HELL
LONDON --1980

"Hello? Operator? Long distance lift please."
"Where to sir?"
"Perth, Western Australia."
"Who is paying for the call?"
"I am."
"What's the number?"
"08 644476."

"Hello Suzy, it's Bon."
"Hi Bon, where are you?" The sound of her voice breaks my heart.
"I'm in London, we flew back from New York yesterday."
"Must be about three in the morning there" she says.
"Yeah, something like that. I can't sleep."
"Are you drunk, Bon?"

"I've had a few shandies darling, you know me."

"Bon, please, don't call me darling, or baby. I can tell you're drunk. I told you not to ring me when you're drunk. You always upset me."

"But I'm lonely." There's a pause. I hear her sigh. I imagine her sitting on the floor in our apartment in East Fremantle, twisting the phone cord in her fingers.

"I'm sorry I missed you when you were here," she says.

"What are you talking about?"

"I forgot about our lunch. You came to our house, we were out. The neighbours said you practically smashed the door off the hinges." My brain hurts. Was a drunken week. I *thought* we met.

"Bon? Do you remember? I spoke to you on the phone the next day."

"I don't remember. Guess you wouldn't have forgotten our lunch if I was Gerald or Jerard, or what's his name?"

"Jim, Bon, his name is Jim. We have a life together now, and a baby. We're a family. You can meet us next time."

"*We* were meant to be a family. You and I were going to travel the world together. We were going to live in a little caravan behind the tour bus. Remember? I waited for you. I even went to fuckin' church for you." I finish my whisky.

"No you didn't, Bon, don't pull that with me." Anger enters her voice. "You married five years ago, that hurt me too. You had your chance, Bon. It's over."

"I'm single now. In two years I'll quit touring and we can live together, like we always said. I'm moving back to Freo, I looked at property when I was there." She doesn't answer. I catch myself in the mirror.

"What's the matter, Bon?"

"Nothing."

"Why are you ringing then?"

"Just wanted to say hello, isn't that what friends do? Did you get my letter? I love you, Tweety."

"I know, Bon. I love you too, but we can't be together. You remember when I came to Melbourne? Years ago? When you were living in Dalgety Street?"

"Yeah," I say.

"You remember you sent me the Jones letter?"

"Yeah."

"I got it, Bon, before I left. I lied and said I didn't get it. I didn't have the heart to break it off."

"You're joking?" I laugh. "You'll see, the band is breaking in the States, I'll be a millionaire. I'll buy you anything you want. I did it, Suzy." I grab a fistful of bed sheet.

"I'm happy for you, Bon, but you need help. You have a drinking problem."

"Why don't you want to be with me then?" I pour another whisky. My eyes water.

"Bon, this is Jim. Look mate, we're going to have to let you go."

"Oh. Hi Gerald."

"You're upsetting Suzy, mate. Piss off and leave us alone."

He hangs up. A few minutes pass. I listen to the beeps. *Hello. This is the operator. The other line has disconnected, sir.*

Loud spraying noise outside. I pull a pillow over my ear. Dream of running. Dream of not being able to run. Spraying noise is louder. Just below my window. I open the blind in the bay window. Glass covered in frost. I wipe with my hand. In the blur I see a couple of geezers wearing dirt covered denim jeans and jackets. One sprays, one sweeps. They have the casualness of people who have been doing the same job for years. Birds chirp. In the window frost I write the word S-O-N-G. Must write a song today. Just one song.

If not a song, a verse. If not a verse, a title. Have a few ideas. *Rock and Roll Aint Noise Pollution.* Came up with that one after the caretaker told us to turn the music off one night. Another title, *Let Me Put My Love Into You.* Quite proud of that one. Still need lyrics. Always the same story, struggling through the motions.

I flick through my notebook again and again. I listen to my favourite albums. The bar is raised this time. Less stealing allowed. Everyone is watching. Needs to be *me*. Needs to be the lyrics people expect, but better, cleaner, wittier.

My eyes sting from lack of sleep. I pour myself a throat concoction. I stand at the window and the street lights turn off. I make coffee. I pace the apartment. I hum a few lines from Malcolm's riff. Just need the first line, the rhythm, the length, the rhyming pattern, the theme of the song. To be clever takes time. To turn a phrase, to elevate a *double entendre* above a cliche requires an image, a real place to ground the chorus.

Oh, why am I talking to you? You don't care. You just wanna hear the finished product. I know what you're thinking, you're thinking, *Quit your bleating, you wanker, I gotta get up at six every morning and go to work on a building site and bust my gut six days a week. Just make some great albums and get on with it.*

I sweep the apartment floor, collect all my dirty clothes, do the dishes, change the bed sheets, wipe the oven, order my albums, put the books back on the shelf, make more coffee, have a shit and shave. Ring Mum. "Yes Mum, I'll be back later in the year. I know. Yes, trying to eat better. No, not drinking so much. Glad you like the last album Mum. I'll buy you and Dad a new house after the next album. It's called *Back in Black*. These things take time Mum. Absofuckinglutely. Sorry. How's work at the uni? How is she? Send my love. I know, only a few years left. How did the choir show go? The choir, you told me you had a show coming up. No need to be coy about it. Don't need a will Mum, not dying anytime soon. Do you have to be so morbid? Hang on Mum, wait. I'll call you back."

A line. A line! Yes. Okay. Okay, now another. Something like that Alex Harvey line about gonorrhoea. No, done that to death. Pub? No, not yet. Concentrate. Wank? Always get a boner when I need to write. Write Bon, *for fuck's sakes.* Malcolm and Angus having a blow today. Go along later and play drums and piece together more songs. We have some ideas from before *Highway to Hell.*

I'M SAD WHEN I SHOULD BE HAPPY
I SEE THE WAVE, THE BYE-BYE.
ALL OF YOU SEE, ALL OF YOU CAN SEE,
LET THEM WALK WHILE I ENJOY MYSELF.

Not bad. No good for an AC/DC song though.

I grab the phone and dial. "Hi Silver. Let's go out for dinner, I want to celebrate."

"Celebrate what?" she asks.

"I did it. I've been writing all day. I wrote most of the lyrics. I want to have dinner with you. Somewhere in Covent Garden?"

"I don't know, Bon. We're not meant to be seeing each other, remember?" Her voice sounds strained.

"Come on, just for dinner. Forget about everything else."

"Alistair is here. He might want to join you. You been drinking?"

"Alistair? He never goes out..."

"I know, but Anne is in hospital...He's nodding, he'll go out with you, he'll probably drive too."

"Okay, so you're not coming?"

"They got me, Bon."

"Who?"

"The cops. They took my stash and my money."

"Oh. Bummer."

"Lost the deposit for my house. Might have to go back to Adelaide. And I've been reading this book and was lying in bed too long, think I might have pulled a nerve or something."

"Why did you leave me at the station?"

"You left yourself at the station, you idiot," she protests. "You passed out after you ate the block of hash. You were walking around in circles, and falling over and blacking out. I missed the Stones because of you, you dick. I might be a junkie, but I never pull that shit."

"I'm sorry."

She moans. I think about lying with her on her sofa, looking up at the painting on the wall.

"You have to think about other people from time to time, you know. You can't get out of it whenever you feel like it."

"I know, Silver, I'm trying. I've been seeing the doctor about my liver."

"What's he saying?"

"He says if I stay off the booze it'll repair itself."

"You been off the booze?"

"Not really," I laugh.

"I'm no better," she says. "Can't stay off the shit no matter what I try."

"I'll shout you dinner, anywhere you want."

"I'll see, Bon. I'm stressed out a bit, haven't been the best company lately."

"Okay, I'll see ya later then."

"Hey Alistair, where are you?" I take a gulp of whisky.

"Hi Bon, yeah, I'm in Dulwich now, going to leave soon. You had dinner?"

"I don't feel like eating. Meet me at my place we can go to the Music Machine after?"

"Alright, Bon. Where do you live?"

"You've been to my place, haven't you? In Westminster?"

"Oh yeah." He hangs up. Never been the most talkative bloke. *Open the phone booth. Feel sick. Fucking stand up.*

If you're reading this, then I'm not in hell. *That word.* Hell. H, E, double L. Has a million and one meanings. A different meaning for each person. Their own personal hell. People fight over its meaning. Some people think hell is all fire and fry. I bet they only have cold coffee.

Hell is a state of mind. A place of punishment. Trapped. You can be in hell without doing anything wrong. Those poor bastards in chain gangs, the slaves and convicts who lived with the blues, who were not allowed to love. Hell is born in the blues. Or blues born in Hell? Those poor bastards working for nothing, living someone else's lie. The non-existent punishments that won't let you go. Like your lover who tells you to piss off, making you more trapped. This restless state of mind. The longing heart. Oh, I had a woman, a beautiful woman, but she left me. You come to grips. You bite the bullet and start again. The blues at your fingertips. I hope rock and roll never leaves me.

Hey Alistair. Cauliflower John. The Music Machine.

I've written hundreds of songs about hell. Most will never see the light of day. At first I felt bad about using H.E.L.L., but when no one said anything I kept singing about it, going deeper and deeper. Why should religion control the word? My mum goes to church every Sunday, she's a Christian. Maybe I'm a Christian? Throw me to the lions. Life and death, heaven and hell, someone's breath, someone's bell. Mum knows I don't pray, but she prays for me.

My friends think I'm lucky. I guess I'm lucky. I've traveled most of the world, played to millions of people. I've said it before and I'll say it again, it's hard work and very few people are cut out for it. Most singers would only last a week doing what I do. Most people would say I'm lazy. A bum musician who offers nothing. A lay-about. A draft-resisting loafer. I tried the nine to five thing. You can stick your golden hand-shake. No way. Bye bye. What's the point?

Gotta piss. Get up. Hold on. Great band.

I've had to rely on other people far too often. I've always given everything I've had to give. If someone needs ten bucks and I have ten bucks they can have it, don't bother me. You have to look after each other, everyday. People are more important than money. One day when I'm filthy rich, I'll prove that to everyone.

Musicians are the only ones who do well out of war. On the other hand, people are out there killing each other and critics want to be your enemy because they don't like your music. Who's thinking wrong? When we have our fans in our hands, we don't start a riot, we laugh in the pigs' faces.

"Fuck off Alistair, you want a drink or not? Make it a double. A double."

Some people say you should steer clear of cliches. I go straight for them. Cliches are there for us to play with, to tangle, to mould. If you can give a cliche a new meaning, you're getting close. To give a cliche a new meaning brings new light to the old meaning. The duality. The opposites working together. The *double entendre*, as the French say.

Take me. There's the me that I am, and the me that I want to be. I see myself in different guises. One that stands out is the me where I'm lying on my bed, any day of the week, listening to my stereo as loud as possible. Going for broke, jumping the springs flat. Not this rock music without the noise nonsense. The real deal, you know.

I'm in North Freo. Mum, Dad and my brothers are out. I pull back the curtains on the bay windows. Right then the ships in the port toot in some naval chorus singing, "Gday Bon, how you doing, old son?" I look to the south, across the blue river, over the cliffs, to Terry's house, shooting down grassy hills with the bastard. I look to Suzy's. She's there with her baby, and Gerald. To Wyn and Ted and the boys. Even Vince, the cunt. Then I look east to Bruce and Irene and Fraternity and Malcolm and Angus and all that is AC/DC.

I pour myself a bourbon and lick up a jazz cigarette. Soon the table's spinning and the first few loops of vinyl come to life, like a reel to reel taking hold. The perfect moment when the power of music is infinite. A power every record shares. That crackling big-bang. If you listen close enough every record has the musos reaching for the stars. When all the pain and suffering and hell are forgotten. Where all the hang ups and negative comments and doubts and fears and violence have no place. Where all the people who have given up, or never given the chance, or had their chance taken away from them, they too feel alive and free and happy. Here there is no life or death, no afterlife. No hot war, no cold war, no one telling you what to do.

Eh? Cold metal. Frosted windows. Engine noise. Put me down. Put me down. Alistair. Alistair, don't worry. I'll sleep it off.

Yeah, I've been to hell, ya know. It ain't such a bad place. To open your heart to someone and have it torn apart makes you wanna cry. Invites the devil around for lunch. Every show I play, you see it in their eyes. The devil running amok in their hearts and heads. Kids staring into your soul searching for answers. The most dreadful sickness has trapped them. They turn to you for advice and I pretend to be strong and have answers and have a drink and give an autograph and shake their hand and have another drink and hopefully their worries have disappeared for a moment. And if they have disappeared it's time to drink some more. Like the preacher, fail at God's work and you can blame the devil.

That you, mum? Why are we driving? Thought the mini was in getting fixed?

I close my eyes. My right arms stings. I'm not dancing. Well, I'm not dancing the way I want to. Inside I'm dancing. I can feel their eyes on me. My stomach expands and contracts. I feel the hole in my shoe as my toes clench. Everyday seems a little longer, everyday love's a little stronger, come what may. Do you ever long for true love from me? For a moment I glimpse a warm place filled with love and music. There's a house with a garden and a swimming pool and slippery dips and diving boards and a playground for everyone. We grow our own food and work the land when we need to. My wife is beautiful and we have many children who we love. In winter we tour to warmer climates. There's a big tour bus with all our gear. Every band member has a small bus with their families. We tour the world. We bring happiness. We have toured Australia so many times the road house owners know us by name and are happy to see us. We travel and swap our music for food and fuel. You'll see us ride out on the sunset, the black shapes of our buses getting smaller and smaller. Eventually just the sound of our music and the memory of joy. I open my eyes, half expecting to be punched out or jeered at. But the room is empty. Everyone has left. Almost as if no one was here in the first place. The lights are turned off. The windows closed. My thoughts drift back to the song. I hum the melody. I restart the tune and get it right the second time. Now I can dance properly. I run to the front of the room and take a flying leap. I grab the blackboard duster and pretend it's a microphone. I work the crowd and ask them to join in clapping. When I know we're working as one I return to the band and resume the song. I'm unstoppable. Everyone loves me. Those that hate me envy me. Those who're indifferent know who I am. I am Bon Scott. The greatest rock and roll singer who ever lived. Everywhere I go there is a party. Everywhere I go the music is good and the music is loud. Other musicians come and go. New fads come and go but I'm still here. I'll be here because I believe in myself. I don't need no psychiatrist or what you call 'em. You just keep going. One band falls apart, you start a new band. A bass player gets married you find another one. Each album unique. Each sound the culmination of our friendship. When you're mad you sing like you're about to die. You keep going no matter what. The long roads keep going and so should you. You get chased out of a town for sleeping with the mayor's daughter and laugh until your ribs hurt.

EPILOGUE

Ronald Belford Scott died on the nineteenth of February 1980, aged 33.

The coroner's report stated the cause of death as acute alcohol poisoning and death by misadventure.

Scott's memorial in Fremantle is the most visited in Australia.

ACKNOWLEDGMENTS

Gratitude to my mentors and friends, John Kinsella and Stephen Chinna, for their patient advice, comment and encouragement.

Thank you to my partner, Rosemary Halsmith.

Thank you to Bon Scott's friends who opened their doors and hearts. In no particular order: Maria Short, Murray Gracie, Bruce Howe, 'Uncle' John Ayres, Carol Anderson, John Freeman, Fifa Riccabono, Silver Smith, Gabby and Darcy, Michael Browning, Sue Lovegrove, Chris Gilbey, Peter Head, Rob (Ralph) and Theresa Booth, Martin Johnson, Ian Meldrum, Paul Drane, John Bissett, Vicki De Bellis and Mary Renshaw.

To Clinton Walker, Jesse Fink and Tim Fisher for their time. The idea for the letters found herein are derived from Walker's book, *Highway To Hell.*

Thank you to my friends and family for support and dialogue — Neil and Julie Collins, Maureen Murray, Stanley Bill, Mathew Hall, Lorenz Gude, Jim Mitchell, Keith Ashbolt, James Ricks, Paul Clifford, Shane Starling, Lee Garret and Peter Stafford.

Thanks to the Welke family for the roof over my head.

Thank you to Alan Sanders and Alan Dawson for providing access to Riverbank Detention Centre.

Thank you to Philip Adams for the use of the Barry Mckenzie lyrics.

Thank you to Allan Handelman for being great and for the use of the interview.

Thank you to Justin Quinton who encouraged me to listen to Bon Scott. Rock in peace brother.

About the Author

James P. Quinton is a writer and adventurer. The idea for *Bad Boy Boogie* came to him while cycling around the United Kingdom for nine weeks in 2011. Before that he studied Landscape Architecture and worked for an environmental company in Perth, Western Australia. He is now writing his next novel about hiking in Japan, New Zealand and North America.

Visit James' website at www.jpquinton.com

Made in the USA
Lexington, KY
06 December 2018